THE EDGE

THE EDGE

a novel

DICK BARBIERI

iUniverse, Inc.
Bloomington

The Edge

This is a work of fiction. All of the characters, names, incidents, organizations, and dialogue in this novel are either the products of the author's imagination or are used fictitiously.

iUniverse books may be ordered through booksellers or by contacting:

iUniverse
1663 Liberty Drive
Bloomington, IN 47403
www.iuniverse.com
1-800-Authors (1-800-288-4677)

Roberta J. Buland, Editor

ISBN: 978-1-4620-2645-6 (sc)
ISBN: 978-1-4620-2646-3 (hc)
ISBN: 978-1-4620-2647-0 (e)

Library of Congress Control Number: 2011912164

Printed in the United States of America

iUniverse rev. date: 08/25/2011

"You can become a winner only if you are willing to walk over the edge."
Damon Runyon

CHAPTER ONE

A s Angie awoke to the warm, tropical sunlight shining through the open window and the sound of the surf off in the distance, she wondered what time it was. Then, she thought, she did not care. They were on vacation. It was a special vacation.

She and her husband, Aldo, were celebrating their wedding anniversary and had returned to the place where they had honeymooned 25 years ago. It was a small Caribbean island in the British West Indies. They were staying at the same beach house where they had spent their first week of marriage, even though it was quite a bit more expensive now, and they had to use some of their savings to pay for it. But, it was a beautiful spot and they both figured it was well worth it, and that they deserved it. It was a raised beach house, with panoramic views off the large patio of one of the most beautiful beaches in the world. The powdery white sand and pristine blue-green water was perfect for snorkeling or scuba diving among the many coral reefs. Yet, it was a quiet little island, still undiscovered by most tourists.

Angie thought about her husband and felt for him next to her. When he was not there, she knew he had already gone for his morning walk, as he had done every morning, both here and at home on Long Island. She smiled to herself when she recalled how wonderful last night had been. They had gone for dinner to celebrate their wedding date at a little local restaurant with a beautiful sunset view. They stayed past sunset, walked home hand in hand, and then they made glorious love, as good as when they were newlyweds, but made even better by 25 years of commitment and experience.

She lingered in bed for a few more minutes, savoring the moment, then got out of bed. She looked for her robe but then thought, why bother since she was alone, and headed naked toward the bathroom. That was when she noticed the folded note on the vanity next to the bed. Wow, she thought, he left me a love note. Tears of joy were starting as she slowly opened the letter.

"My dear Angie," it started. "Last night was wonderful and I hope you remember us like that forever. I have some terrible news, and I hope you forgive me for telling you like this. When I went to doctor Mangio last month for my stomach problems, he sent me for some tests. Then he sent me for more. I didn't want to scare you so I didn't tell you. Last week he told me I have cancer that is spreading fast. He gives me maybe six months. No chance of remission. We have no health insurance since the company went under and six months of fighting a losing battle would destroy us financially. You would be left with nothing. No house, nothing. I do have my life insurance, double indemnity in case of an accident, $500,000. Please forgive me, but I have decided to die at my own time, in the place I love, the ocean. This is my wish, please help me see it through. Destroy this note. No one can ever see it. Wait awhile, then call the constable, tell him I haven't returned from my walk. Please do this! Live a good life, remember us as we were last night.. I LOVE YOU, GOODBYE, ALDO"

For a moment Angie was paralyzed. Her brain was shocked and confused. Then what she had just read hit her and she almost lost consciousness. She recovered momentarily and ran out onto the patio. "Aldo!!" she screamed. She then realized that she was naked and quickly went back into the house. She found a shirt on the floor and pulled it over her head as she stumbled down the patio stairs and headed toward the beach.

A half a mile away, Aldo sat on the beach, contemplating his last hurrah. He thought about the events that had led him to this point, to the fatal decision he had made and was now about to carry out. Ten months earlier he had begun to feel cramps and bloating in his stomach that he thought were due to the stress he was going through when his company began failing. For a while he took antacids and other over the counter medications which would temporarily ease the problem. Angie kept insisting that he see a doctor but he kept putting it off. He thought it was an ulcer. He lost his appetite and began losing weight. It was then that he finally went to see his doctor, who sent him for a series of tests. When he finally got the news he had feared, he anguished over how to tell his wife. He knew she would be devastated and he did not want to put her through the hell of watching helplessly as he slowly died. He hid the pain, made excuses and lied to Angie that the test results were still incomplete. It was a nightmare. It was soon after that he made the decision that brought him here, to the point where he would end his life. He had gone through it in his mind many times. There was a spot on a hill up the beach where a small platform had been built years ago to view the sunset and the catamaran races the natives held on holidays. It was on a cliff 100 feet above the ocean, with jagged rocks below. He had calculated the time the tide would be highest so if the fall didn't kill him, he could never survive the rough sea and strong currents. The observation platform, only 12 feet wide and 16 feet long, had been abandoned and closed to tourists a few years ago when the cliffs below started to erode and it became unsafe to stand up there.

It was still early in the day, so the beach was deserted. He would run along the beach, up the path straight to the deck, slip past the barrier and run right off the edge. Good bye and good luck! When his body washed ashore, it would look like an accident, like he fell off. He only hoped that Angie and his doctor could keep his secret. His stomach cramped, the pain reminding him of what he had to do. He got up and started to run, hoping that by the time he got to his ending point, he would be so out of breath that he would lose consciousness during the fall. He ran faster and faster up the path. Getting closer and closer, panting, gasping, he bounded onto the platform, over the edge!!

When Angie reached the beach she did not know which way to turn. She ran up the beach 100 yards, stopped, turned the other way and started running back, not knowing which way her husband had gone. She screamed again. "No, Aldo, please, no!!"

She started running again, stumbled and fell to the sand, her heart racing. She saw that she still clenched the note in her hand. She opened it and read the words again. "This is my wish, please help me see it through. Please do this!!" She put her arms around her head and started to cry hysterically.

"Why, why, why didn't he tell me?" She tried to get up, but fell back down. After minutes of sobbing and agonizing, she realized it was most likely too late to save him. When he was determined to do something, he usually had a flawless plan, and executed it perfectly. Now, hopelessly, she thought, if this is what he wanted, she must do her part to make sure it ends as he had planned.

She got up, looked again in both directions and then toward the sea. She walked slowly into the water. When it was up to her waist, she tore the note into tiny pieces, dove below the surface and scattered the pieces along the ocean floor. She wished she could stay down and be with him there forever, but her natural instincts pulled her to the surface. She swam in, and slowly made her way back to the house.

CHAPTER TWO

DING!! The attention signal from the cockpit awakened her. "Once again, folks, this is your captain. We are approaching JFK and should be on the ground in about 20 minutes. The weather in New York is overcast, the temperature is 55 degrees. Hope you enjoyed your trip and thanks for flying with us today."

Angie immediately thought about her husband's coffin in the cargo hold. She had done as he wished. She had waited two endless hours, called the constable's office and reported him missing. Someone had already reported a body washed up on the beach on the far side of the island, and they had sent out a team to investigate. The constable had sent an officer to pick her up and bring her to the morgue at the small hospital on the island.

When Angie arrived there she had to wait for what seemed like forever until they brought in the body. She almost could not bear to look at it. It was emaciated from being in the water, and the face had been battered by the rocks, but she was sure it was Aldo and officially identified the body. She had called George and he made the arrangements to get the body back to the states. George Macklin was an old and dear friend. He owned and operated Macklin's Funeral Home in Syosset on Long Island, New York, where Aldo and Angie resided. He and his wife, Freda, were very close friends with Angie and Aldo for as long as she could remember. Freda had died eight years before in a freak accident at home. She liked her martinis and was frequently inebriated. George found her in the pool late one night when he returned from a Rotary Club meeting.

Because George and Aldo were best friends, Angie regretted telling him the news about his death over the phone, but he was the only one she could turn to now. He was shocked by her words, but he told her he would make all the arrangements, and she should just get herself home.

George had told Angie that he would meet her at the airport, but when the flight was delayed, he called to tell her he had a funeral to attend to and could not get there on time. Her car was at the airport so she could drive herself home. She would see him in the morning.

Angie was now 45 years old. Aldo would have been 48 next month. He was the only man she had ever been with. They had met in college, became engaged and married the summer after she graduated. George and Freda were their best man and maid of honor. The four of them had met at The University of Connecticut. (UConn) George and Aldo were from Long Island. Angie came from Connecticut, and Freda was from a military family that had most recently lived in Newport, Rhode Island. Angie and Aldo were always close. George and Freda were on-again, off-again companions, and eventually stayed together long enough to get married. Their marriage was basically the same as their college relationship, but somehow it survived until Freda's untimely accident.

Angie and Aldo had no children. They had tried for a while, considered adoption, but then decided it was not meant to be. She was the youngest of three children and both her siblings had passed away. Aldo was an only child. His parents had returned to Italy a few years after she and Aldo had married. She had not seen them since she and Aldo had gone abroad to visit a few years ago. She would have to try to reach them in the morning, even though she had trouble communicating with them. She spoke little Italian and they little English.

So now, besides George, a few local friends, and a high school girlfriend in Michigan, she had no one. Tears started again when she thought of this.

George would have the body picked up and brought to his facility. She got her luggage and as she walked to her car, the sky opened and it started to pour. She began to cry again and continued as she drove through the rain, back to her empty home.

CHAPTER THREE

The ringing startled her from her light sleep. She awoke, realized that she was at home in her bed, and fumbled for the phone. She saw the clock. It was 6:05 a.m. "Hello," she said.

"Angie, it's George, are you awake?"

"Yes," she said.

"Angie, you've got to come down here, right away!"

"Why, what's the matter?" she mumbled.

"Did you identify the body on the island?"

"Of course. Why?" she said.

"Just get down here now!"

"Ok," she said. "I'm on my way"

Angie threw on jeans and a sweatshirt and drove to Macklin's. It was only ten minutes but it seemed like hours. What could it be, she thought. She had no idea!

When she arrived, she went to the back entrance, past the office and into the mortuary. George was standing near a gurney with a body, covered by a white sheet. He hugged her tightly and said, "I'm so sorry." She embraced him and began to cry again.

"What's the matter, George?" she said softly.

"You saw the body and identified it positively?" he asked.

"Yes, I did," she said. "Why?"

"Well, I can see it's pretty hard to make out the facial features.

Probably was in the ocean for a while. But look here." He removed the sheet from the lower portion of the body to expose the legs. "There's no scar. No V."

Aldo had had a noticeable V-shaped scar on his right leg, just above the ankle. He had gotten it over 25 years ago. They were all at a college party on the beach on Cape Cod. He got drunk and stumbled into the bonfire. His buddies pulled him out quickly, but he had burned his leg. It was in the shape of a V, and they all later laughed that it was Aldo's V for Victory scar that was a lucky charm for the football team. He would raise his leg and expose the scar whenever the team scored a touchdown.

"I never looked for it," said Angie.

"Besides," George said, "this man's shorter than Aldo."

"Oh, my God! It was terribly hard for me to look at him. But I thought it must be him. There must be some way to tell for sure."

"Yes, there are some biological tests, but they will take time."

George paused a moment. "Angie?" he said slowly. "Aldo confided in me about the way he wanted to die, if he ever got terminally ill. I can't help thinking this was it. We had that talk just before you went away. He didn't say he was that sick, but." She felt the air go out of her. She remembered his note and did not know what to say. He saw by her expression that she thought he may be right.

"Maybe we should think this over," he said. "If I know Aldo, he took care of the business side of this, you know, insurance. At least, I hope he did. So one of our, I mean, your options is to have this body cremated. That was also his wish, right? I will do the paperwork and you can collect any insurance money he wanted you to have."

"Oh no," she said. "How do we know who this is? Someone might be looking for this person! What if Aldo's body shows up?"

"We'll probably never know who this is, could have come from anywhere in the Caribbean. But, I can find out over the Internet if any unclaimed bodies show up down there. Then, I can go down, claim the body and bring him back. We could then cremate the body as he wished. But most likely the body will never be found."

She couldn't think straight. She had to sit down.

"I think he would have wanted you to do this Ang," he said.

"I don't know," she said. "I have to think about it."

"Well, OK," he said, "but you shouldn't wait too long."

CHAPTER FOUR

A ngie started for home. Her head was spinning. She and George had agreed to meet later in the day to talk about the final arrangements, if she agreed to the plan. She lived in the Muttontown section of Syosset. On the way she passed the Locust Street Cemetery, where her friend Freda was buried. She parked on the car path next to Freda's plot. It was still early morning, and there was no one else around. There was a light fog and mist seemed to be rising from the ground as a result of a late night down pour. It was very quiet, almost eerie, and it had a strange, calming effect on Angie. She sat in her car, rolled the window down and thought about Aldo and her old friends.

It was 1968 when they first met. Freda was a junior at UConn and Angie, a sophomore transfer from a community college in New Haven, Connecticut. Freda's roommate had dropped out, and Angie was assigned to share a room with her. At first Freda was resentful they had given her a new roommate, never mind a transfer who was away from home for the first time, nerdy and shy. Freda had many partying friends on campus but, although she tried, could not get her new roommate interested in any of her extracurricular activities. Angie was homesick and became a weekend warrior, traveling back and forth to her hometown, only an hour and a half away, as often as she could.

Just before Thanksgiving break that year, Angie recalled, Freda and her friends threw a keg party in the basement of their dorm and insisted Angie stay on campus and come to the party. She also remembered Freda calling her a geek and insisting she get a social life, somehow, or she would drive her crazy.

Angie smiled to herself as she recalled Freda's pep talk.

"Come on girl, you've got to loosen up. You might even meet someone you like," Freda insisted.

"There's gonna be a lot of jocks there." Reluctantly, Angie agreed.

The girlfriends in the dorm started getting ready for the party as soon as classes ended for the day. They rearranged the furniture in the basement activity room, hung decorations, set up the music, shopped for snacks and made Jell-O shots. Around five, a few of their boyfriends snuck two kegs of beer into the dorm. Alcohol was legally not allowed on campus, but it was easy to get it, and as long as there was not any trouble, these parties were generally overlooked by campus security. At eight o'clock, their guests started arriving.

Angie was sitting in the corner when George Macklin and Aldo Ferrari walked in. George was a linebacker on the football team, and Aldo was on the swim team. They had similar facial features and could be mistaken for brothers, although George was a bit taller and more heavyset. They were roommates, fraternity brothers and popular on campus. George was more outgoing, even a little cocky, and with his good looks and athletic build, had plenty of coed admirers, Freda being the most ardent. Aldo was more reserved, but still took advantage of his popularity and the crowd that George drew. They went directly to the keg and as they passed Angie, Aldo gave her a nod and said "Hi". She liked him immediately but looked away, thinking she had seen him on campus somewhere but was not sure where. After getting a beer, the two friends split up and George started working the room.

A little later, when Angie was helping put out the chips and pretzels, she bumped into Aldo again. He actually bumped into her, knocking the pretzels to the floor. While he was helping her with the mess, Aldo asked, "Aren't you in my history class? At two on Tuesdays and Thursdays?"

She gave him a close look and said, "Yes, I think so, it's such a large class. I don't know everyone, you know."

"Yeah, Professor Brady. Some of that stuff he comes up with is pretty wild."

"It is kind of interesting," Angie said.

They moved to the side of the room, away from the dancers as "Jumpin' Jack Flash" blared from the speakers. They chatted for a while, had a few beers and as the party started to get rowdy, Aldo asked her if she wanted to go for coffee at the Student Union a few blocks away. She thought about it and then declined. After all, she thought, she just met him, and who knew what he had in mind after a few beers. He did not persist, and after he said he would call her, she went upstairs to her room to get her things ready to go home for vacation.

She opened the door to her room, flicked on the light and was startled by George coming out of the bathroom, stark naked. Freda sat up in the bed and yelled, "You could have knocked!!."

Angie slammed the door shut and ran down the hallway and down the stairs, just as Aldo was going out the front door. "Change your mind?" he asked.

"What? Yeah, sure. Let's go," she blurted out. Little did Angie know that this was the man that would eventually make her Mrs. Aldo Ferrari.

After that first semester and a few more tense episodes, Freda and Angie became close friends, with Aldo and George as boyfriends. When the boys married their college sweethearts, the Ferraris and Macklins settled near each other on Long Island, New York.

The caretaker at the cemetery beeped the horn on his van as he tried to pass by Angie's car that was blocking the path. She was startled back to reality. Angie wiped the tears from her face, blew Freda a kiss and pulled out of the driveway.

At home, Angie started the task of going through her late husband's possessions. Every item, every picture brought more tears and sobbing. She remembered the note he had left her. "Please help me see it through." The words kept pounding in her head.

CHAPTER FIVE

"L.I. MAN DIES IN CARIBBEAN DROWNING ACCI-DENT" read the headline in the New York Post.

"Syosset resident Aldo Ferrari died last week in Anguilla when he apparently fell into the ocean while taking an early morning walk. He was alone at the time and his wife of twenty-five years, Angela, reported him missing when he did not return. His body was discovered a short time later by a local fisherman along the shore. Mr. and Mrs. Ferrari were on vacation at the time.

Funeral services will be private".

After much thought, Angie agreed to go along with George's plan. The body was cremated. The obit was released and a short service held. All the legal work was completed and, a month later, Angie received a check from Northwest Mutual Insurance for $500,000. Aldo had made sure his will was in order, leaving everything they had to her. Her attorney advised her to have a will drawn up for herself and so she did, leaving 20 percent of her assets to The American Cancer Society in memory of Aldo and naming her closest friend, George Macklin, as beneficiary. She tried to go on with her life.

CHAPTER SIX

Just before Aldo hit the water, he drew what he thought would be his last breath. He plunged into the sea and went straight down, miraculously missing the rocks he suspected would end his life. He immediately felt the undertow dragging him out to sea. As a natural reaction, he held his breath as long as he could and then succumbed to his body's demand for oxygen.

Two young native boys were in their small boat doing what they did most mornings, checking on their family's crayfish traps. To Eduardo, 17, and Melky, 13, it was a chore they were assigned by their father and the earlier they got it done, the more time they had during the day for fun. They would haul up the traps, harvest anything edible, reset the bait and go on to the next one. The ten traps took them about an hour if they hurried, but most days they took their time. The crayfish and crabs would be sold or bartered for other things their family needed, or end up on the family dinner table.

The boys were rowing their craft from one trap to the next. About 30 yards away, Aldo first bobbed to the surface. Melky saw it first and was unsure of what it was. He motioned to Eduardo, but when they looked again, it was gone. But, when it came up again, the older boy saw it and realized it was a body. He maneuvered the boat closer, and when it was within reach, he grabbed onto an arm with a fishing line they kept on the boat. They both pulled the body aboard as seawater gushed from Aldo's mouth and nose. When the boys realized they could be performing a rescue, they started rowing frantically toward shore.

The boys lived in a small village on the far end of the island. It consisted of a dozen shacks where as many families lived. It was about seven miles from any other village, via dirt roads. The people lived a kind of primitive lifestyle. They were a self-sufficient tribe that lived off the land and the sea, having very little contact with the rest of the island. They were descendants from the Arawak tribe that originally inhabited the island until the British arrived in 1650. While most of the tribe had been eradicated by the invading Redcoats, this small group managed to survive by hiding out in the rain forest that bordered their seaside village. Now, centuries later, they still kept to themselves, only occasionally venturing to other parts of the island. However, although they had learned to speak the English language now used by most of the islanders, they were still looked down upon as a lower class.

When the brothers got their craft back to shore, Melky ran to get his father as Eduardo looked after Aldo, who by now was vomiting seawater and blood.

The father, Arote, arrived with two other men. They lifted Aldo out of the boat and placed him on his side on the sandy beach. They let him continue to rid his body of foreign substances before sitting him up. He was still gasping for air when one of the men shoved a leaf soaked in a strange liquid under his nose. Instinctively, he took one long, deep breath and his breathing returned to normal. His first thought was that he had failed. He had tried to end his life, and he was still alive. He immediately thought of Angie. How had she taken his decision? Had she followed his instructions? If she did, the authorities would now be looking for him. Where was he? Who were these people? He took another deep breath.

One of the older men spoke. "What happened, mon?" he said. "Did you fall off your boat?"

"Uh, no," Aldo said. "I was swimming, the current was very strong. Where are we?"

The men looked at each other as if they were reluctant to answer him. "Where were you swimming?" one asked.

Aldo thought about his situation. Did he really want to be returned to where he came from? Maybe he could stay lost and try again to end it all. That way, his plan could still be fulfilled and Angie would claim the insurance money. He rubbed his eyes and forehead and said, "I'm not sure. I'm a little confused right now. Am I still on St. Maarten?"

"Oh, no, mon, this is not St. Maarten." They spoke to each other in a different language. Then one said, "Come, we will take you to my home. There you can rest until you decide what to do. Maybe your head will clear; you will remember where you came from."

CHAPTER SEVEN

George Macklin had been part of Angie's life for over 30 years. She and Aldo had been there for him when Freda had died tragically. Now he was Angie's consoler and tried to be with her as much as possible. He helped her dispose of Aldo's personal belongings, his car, his clothes, and his golf equipment. After a while, it seemed he tried to help her also dispose of his memory.

George took Angie out to dinner and an occasional movie. He ate over at her house often. He stayed over many times because she was worried about him driving home after consuming too much Scotch. He asked her about selling her house and moving in with him. She said it was much too soon and she was beginning to enjoy her independence. He gave her a job at the funeral home as a receptionist, even though he did not need one.

But, George had some secrets. His business was not doing well, and debts were starting to mount up. Even though Macklin's Funeral Home had been in business for many years, it relied on repeat business from the old families that his father, George Macklin, Sr., had gained the respect and trust of. When he passed away, he left the business to George, his only son. Along the way, however, George Jr. had made some enemies. When he was on the planning and zoning board, he voted against some projects that the Signore Construction Company wanted approved. One was a very lucrative project. Geno

Signore tried to influence George, but because George had had a run-in with the younger Signore, Michael, he cast the deciding vote against and the project was rejected.

Geno wanted to have George killed, but since it was such a high profile news item, he decided the best he could do was destroy George's business. He could have had the facility destroyed, but he wanted to put him out of business for good.

Geno made sure Macklin's buried no more of his family, or any other connected Italian family in town. He also did something more devastating. Tony, a young mortician that was working for George, was looking to start his own funeral home, but he could not arrange the financing. Geno was more than willing to set him up, a half mile from Macklin's.

George had another problem. He liked to gamble. It was close to being an addiction. Angie knew he went to Atlantic City or the Connecticut casinos at least once a week, but she never suspected the amounts of money he was wagering. On occasion, when she went with him, he would play blackjack for low stakes. When he was alone, he played the high roller, sometimes winning, but most times losing, $5,000 to $10,000 at a clip. When his business was flourishing, he could afford these losses. But now, with his funds diminishing, he was becoming desperate.

One night, during dinner, Angie asked George about his finances. She had seen a lot of the letters he received, many of which were from collection agencies. As receptionist, she had fielded a few nasty phone calls from people looking for money. She had given him the messages, but he seemed to shrug them off. She had always kept out of his business, but lately it had been hard to avoid. She decided to confront him.

"What's going on?" she asked, sternly.

"Well," George said, "things have been a little slow, especially since that bastard Tony opened over on Third Avenue. I would like to remodel, but I'm having trouble getting the financing. I've never really advertised, never had to. Maybe it would help, but that costs money, too."

"Could I help?" she asked. "You know I have the insurance money."

Of course, George knew. He had helped her get it and it was always in the back of his head as to how he could get his hands on it. Now he had his opportunity.

"No," he said, halfheartedly. "That's for your security. That's what Aldo wanted."

"It would only be a loan," Angie said. "I'm sure Aldo would have wanted to help you. We would draw up all the legal papers. How much would you need to get straightened out?"

Numbers and dollar signs raced through George's head. "Well, I was trying to get $50,000 from the bank."

"I could certainly afford that," she said. "I'd be glad to help. After all," she joked, "I can consider it as job security."

Before the papers were ready, George convinced her to write him a check. He opened a new account at the bank and withdrew $20,000 and headed for Atlantic City.

CHAPTER EIGHT

George arrived in Atlantic City at 5:30 p.m. and immediately checked into Caesar's. Of course, the room was free of charge because of the dollars he had been wagering lately. George had told Angie he was going to a trade show to look for new fixtures for the business. After getting settled, he found a blackjack table and started out with $100 wagers. At first, he was winning and was up two grand when things again turned bad. He was down $5,000 when he changed tables and upped his bets to $500 a clip. That didn't help. He changed tables. The new dealer was hotter than the last one. He would stay at 19, she would hit 20. He would double down, and she would deal herself twenty-one. He finally got up and went to the bar. He had lost $16,000.

While looking for a seat at the bar, George noticed an old high school pal sitting at a table in the far corner of the room. Butch Rogers was engaged in conversation with another patron at the time and didn't seem to notice George walk in. Butch and George had both been linemen on the football team. Butch now worked for a "finance company" that arranged loans for certain needy people. Of course the terms of the loans were rather strict, and nonpayment had very harsh penalties. George had used Butch's services on occasion when he needed some quick cash and did not have time to go through usual channels. He had always made good on his chits and was on good terms with Butch and his associates.

George downed two quick Johnny Walkers and contemplated his next move. Even though he was down thousands, the gambler in him made him feel like he could make a comeback. He still had the four grand. He knew it was too late at night to get more out of his new bank account. He thought about Butch, but he really did not want to get involved with him. He decided to wait until morning, clear his head and then decide if he should quit and go home. He had another drink and went to a crap table where he quickly lost the $4,000. It wasn't a good night.

George was unable to fall asleep. He was thinking about his losses and knew he should probably go home. He thought he could find a way to cover up the $20,000 loss so Angie would not find out he had gambled away her help. After hitting the mini-bar for a few more Johnny Walkers, he finally fell asleep.

George woke up around 9:30 a.m., went for a walk on the boardwalk and again contemplated what he should do. Once again, his gambler instinct overrode his common sense. He had breakfast and called his bank. There was a branch about 15 minutes away, and George was there by 11:00. He withdrew another $20,000 and headed back to the casino.

It was a long day of ups and downs, but by 9:00 p.m., George was on another major downslide. Since he had not eaten since breakfast, he decided to take a break and went to the lounge for some food. He was about to order a Scotch when Butch sat down beside him. "Hey, pal, been sacking any quarterbacks lately?" Butch said.

"Well, if it isn't everyone's favorite shark?" George replied sarcastically. "How you been?"

"I'm doing fine, but I see you ain't been doing too good."

"You don't miss a thing around here, do you? You guys can smell blood from miles away, can't you?"

"What do you mean? I'm just being friendly, trying to help out an old buddy."

The bartender came over and Butch ordered a Budweiser. "Give my old pal here one, too."

"Thanks," George said. "Johnny Walker Black, rocks."

"Can I be of any help to you tonight?" Butch asked.

"I don't know. I think I've done enough damage."

"Well, OK, but you know how tough it is going home with empty pockets."

George thought about Angie and how she would react when she found out that he had lost the money she had lent him to save his business. "You got 50 large?" he blurted out.

"I gotta make a call on that one," Butch replied. "But you got a good record with us, so I'm betting it could be done. Hang here, I'll be back in a minute."

Butch walked away, leaving his beer. George felt a lump in his throat and ordered another Johnny Walker. "Make it a double," he told the bartender.

Butch returned in about ten minutes. "OK. Here's the deal. I can get you $45,000 in a couple hours. You gotta repay us $5,000 a week for ten weeks starting next week. You can either come down here with it or we'll send someone up. Of course, we know you are a respectable businessman and wouldn't want anything happening in your place."

The terms were better than George thought they would be. Like most gamblers, he was always the optimist, thinking he could come up with the $5,000 a week somehow. He could use his credit cards, sell some of his old equipment, and, of course, his luck would change and he could win it back.

"Sounds good. Where you want to meet?" he said.

"Meet me in the sports book room at 11:00, around the corner. There ain't no games on, so it's pretty empty by then."

"Fine," said George. "Want another beer?"

"Nah," Butch said. "I gotta take a ride."

George asked the bartender for a menu and ordered another drink. Shortly, even before he got his refill, an attractive young woman, who appeared to be in her late twenties, sat down on the chair Butch had vacated. She had that look on her pretty face of someone who had also had a bad night. She started going through her purse, as if looking for some change and mumbling about damn machines.

"Tough night?" George said, almost to himself.

She looked his way. "What? Yeah, damn machine, lost my whole paycheck. $234.00. I hope I have money for the tolls," she said as she rifled through her purse.

The bartender came over with the menu and asked her, "Can I get you something, Miss?"

"Um, I'm not sure."

"I got it," George said. "What'll you have?"

"Well, thanks. I'm Gloria, gin and tonic," she said.

"George," he said, reaching out to shake her hand. "I haven't been exactly too lucky either."

"Oh, yeah, what do you play?"

"Blackjack, sometimes craps."

"I don't understand those games," she said. "I usually win on that machine over in the corner. Not tonight, lost it all. I don't know how I'm getting by the rest of this week. I need gas, too. My credit card is maxed out. I don't know."

At that moment, there was a commotion on the other side of the bar. A security man was talking to a woman wearing too much makeup and a dress that was much too tight. She was obviously propositioning a patron. The guard grabbed her by the arm and escorted her out, as she used a number of obscenities.

"That's a way to make some money," George laughed.

Gloria shot him a fiery look and then cracked a smile, "Yeah, I bet I could make a bundle, too."

"Because you're good or because you're fast?" said George.

Gloria smiled, "Whatever you would want me to be."

When Gloria's gin came, George ordered a sandwich. They chatted a while. George offered her $20 to get her home, but she found some ones and some change in her purse. She thanked him for the drink and the company, got off her chair, and leaned over to give him a peck on the cheek. He leaned back and said, "Is this going to be fast or good?"

"Both," she said and planted a kiss on his open mouth.

Pleasantly surprised, George said, "Wow, say, if you really need some funds, I'm staying in room 1206 tonight."

Gloria smiled and walked away.

George finished his corned beef Reuben, downed his Scotch and headed around the corner to the sports book room. He had already gone over in his mind what he would do with the money. Tomorrow, he would put forty grand back in the bank. He would stop at the wholesale furniture showroom in Newark and put some money down on new furniture for his facility. This would cover his alibi with Angie. That would still give him a little money to try to recover his losses at the blackjack table.

George went into the room and sat down in front of one of the hundred or so TVs that were lined up everywhere in the room. Butch had been right. The room was deserted at this time of the night. George turned his attention to a screen showing a Mets-Giants game from the west coast. He had watched three innings without being able to concentrate on the score when Butch strolled into the room with a Fed-Ex box under his arm. Butch handed him the box.

"Your delivery came in," he said.

George took the box and opened one end. In it were tightly wrapped stacks of $100 bills.

"How do I know it's all there?" George said.

"Well, we're trusting you, ain't we?" Butch retorted. "But if you want to count it, take it back to your room. Call me if there's a problem."

"Alright, Anyway, what's a few grand between friends?" George shot back.

"Here's my number," Butch said, handing him a card. "When you come back here next week, call me. Or if you can't make it, let me know and we'll make some arrangements."

George closed the box and got up. Butch stood and held out his hand. "Nice seeing you again, pal," Butch said. "Have a good week; I'll buy you a Scotch next time."

George shook his hand. "Yeah, sure. See ya."

CHAPTER NINE

George went directly to his room, clenching the box tightly under his arm. He locked the door and went into the bedroom area and shook the money out on the bed. Nine stacks of $100 bills fell out. There were fifty each in a stack, totaling $45,000. These guys are good, he thought, if only he didn't have to pay it back. George stuffed the money back in the box, except for one stack. He counted out ten bills from that stack and put them in his pocket. He was closing up the box when the phone on the night stand rang. He hesitated to answer, and then picked it up. "Hello," George said.

"Hi, it's me, Gloria, you know, from at the bar."

"Oh, hi," he said, "What's going on?"

"Well," she started, almost crying. "I'm really down on this money thing, and I can't afford to lose my whole check like I did. I don't' know how I'm gonna get home. I ain't got gas in my car. They want $15 for parking." She started sobbing.

"Whoa! Wait a minute!" said George. "I told you I could help you."

"I don't want anything for nothing," she said, "You know what we were talking about before, in the bar? I kind a like that idea. You know what I mean?"

"I know exactly what you mean," he said. "Come on up. 1206, we'll talk about it."

"OK, see ya in a couple of minutes."

George hung up and thought, why not? I got some extra cash and I'll be helping a damsel in distress. He chuckled to himself. He quickly picked up the Fed Ex box and went to the in-room safe. The box was too big to fit in, and he would have to set a combination. He knew he did not have much time. Gloria would be up in a minute or two. He went back to the bedroom and opened the bottom dresser drawer. He put the box in and covered it with underwear and jeans that he took out of his travel bag.

George went into the bathroom and ran his electric razor over his face. He quickly gargled with mouthwash and splashed on aftershave lotion. He dug deep into his toiletries bag and found a condom he had been saving for a while. There was a knock on the door.

Gloria looked even sexier than she had downstairs at the bar. Her long auburn hair fell slightly over her face. Her eyes seemed more penetrating, and she had applied a soft luster lipstick to her already sexy lips. Her blouse was unbuttoned, revealing inviting cleavage. George noticed her tight miniskirt and long, shapely legs for the first time as she walked by him into the room. She didn't say a word until George spoke.

"Well, good evening," he said, kind of sheepishly. "Welcome."

"Um, yeah, hi," she replied. "Um, I'm not sure how to do this. I hope I'm not being pushy, but, um, can we take care of the money first?"

"Sure," he said "What do you need?"

"Um, I'd at least like to get what I lost. Well, maybe $200. Is that OK?"

George reached in his pocket and pulled out the wad of hundreds. He peeled off three and said, "Here, I'll give you your tip now because I know you'll be good."

"Um, OK, thanks, I'll try." She took the cash, stuffed it in her purse, and put the purse on the shelf under the mirror near the door. She stepped out of her shoes, dropped to her knees in front of George, and started to undo his belt.

"Whoa, take it easy," he said, "I paid you extra to be good, not fast. Come on, let's have a drink."

They went into the bedroom area and George went to the mini-bar and pulled out a bottle of Beefeaters. He poked around and found some tonic. He grabbed a Johnny Walker, some ice, glasses, and made cocktails. "Here's to a good evening and maybe the start of a new career," he said.

Gloria didn't even smile, but drank down half of the drink at once. She gulped down the rest, put down the glass and dropped her skirt to the floor. She took off her blouse and headed toward the bed. George saw she wasn't wearing a bra, and had on only a pink thong. She pulled down the covers and got in bed. "You coming?" she said.

"Not quite, but almost," he quipped to himself as he got undressed.

They rolled around the bed in a sexual frenzy for a few minutes, climaxing with George's sighs of orgasm. He slowly lifted himself off her and sat up.

She rolled over, seemingly exhausted. George got up and went to finish his drink. He noticed himself in the mirror, naked in the dim light. "Not bad," he said to himself proudly. "For a guy pushing 50 who hadn't had sex in a while."

He went into the bathroom and noticed the condom on the vanity.

"Shit," he said to himself. "Too late now, I hope she's as innocent as she seems." He went back to the bedroom, turned out some lights and went back to the bed. Gloria was sleeping. He lay down next to her thinking that, with some luck, maybe he could get a little extra for his money in the morning. He faded off.

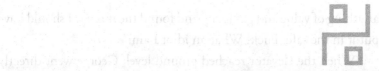

CHAPTER TEN

The morning sunlight, coming in the window and reflecting off the mirror onto George's face, awakened him. He rolled over, feeling for the warm body he had fallen asleep against. He felt nothing. He opened his eyes and realized there was no one in bed with him. He got up and looked around. "Gloria?" he said, waiting for an answer. When there was no reply, he got out of bed and went looking in the bathroom. He relieved himself, and on the way back to the bedroom he noticed her clothes were gone.

"She could have said good bye," he said to himself. Then he noticed that all drawers of the dresser were opened. The clothes in the bottom one were hanging out on the floor. George's heart dropped into his stomach. He bent down and threw everything out of the drawer. No box!! He got up and looked frantically around the room. When he realized he had been robbed, he grabbed his pants, pulled them on, picked up his shirt, and headed for the door. As he did, he realized his pockets were empty. She had taken that cash, too. He found his shoes and ran out of the room into the hallway, hoping to find his "damsel in distress." His mind was racing as he waited alone for the elevator.

"That whore!" he said out loud. "How did she know about the money? Was I set up? Did Butch tell her? That scumbag. I won't pay them. Yeah, right. Maybe she was just looking for jewelry or anything of value and got lucky and found the money. I should have put it in the safe. Fuck! What an idiot I am."

When the elevator reached ground level, George went directly to the bellhop's stand, which was situated with both a view of the elevators and the front doors.

"Can I help you, sir," the man said.

"I hope so. Did you see a young lady, tight dress, maybe with a Fed Ex box come down recently?" George asked.

"Well, I didn't, but I just came on, ten minutes ago, at seven," the man replied,

"Who was on before that? Is he still here?"

"He might be. He'd still be in the office, around the corner if he were. Ask for Fred."

George hurried around the corner, saw the room marked, "Employees only," and tried the door. It did not open so he knocked hard. Another man in bellhop gear came and opened it.

"Can I help you?" he asked.

"Are you Fred?"

"Yes, how can I help you?"

George ran the same questions by Fred.

"Yes, I did see a young lady, quite attractive, come down about three," he said.

"Did she go right out? Did she meet anyone?"

"She went through the casino. I never saw her after that."

"Have you ever seen her around here before?"

"Yes, she was here last night. Made a phone call from the house phone in the lobby. But, I never saw her around here before that," he said. "Why?"

"Uh, she was up to my room, for a drink. She took something she shouldn't have."

"Oh, well, do you want to call the police? File a complaint?"

George thought, "Did he want the police involved? How would

he explain where all that cash came from? Why was it in a box in a drawer and not in the safe? Who was the woman and why was she in his room overnight?" There would be too many questions. Too much publicity.

"No, that's OK," he said. "I'll work it out myself. But, if you ever see her around again, give me a call. Here's my number." He picked up a pen off the desk and wrote his phone number on a pad. "George." he wrote after it.

"I'll make it worth your while if I find her," he told Fred.

George went back to his room and packed his things. Luckily she didn't take his wallet in his jacket, and he still had his credit cards.

The ride back to Long Island was tortuous. He kept running the losses through his head $95,000 in two days. Now he was really desperate! Almost over the edge!

CHAPTER ELEVEN

Aldo drifted in and out of sleep all day and night. He was in a small room in a small cabin near the edge of the village. They had brought him here and laid him on a cot. They told him that when he felt better, they would talk about his future. What to do now that he had failed to end his life was his main concern. He could try it again. How? Where? Could he get away from his new friends? They seemed like they wanted to help him, but they were in no hurry to contact the authorities on the island. Why? What about Angie? Had she followed his plan? Did she hate him now? Could he ever go back to her after what he put her through? If he stayed where he was, how long would it be before the cancer killed him?

The sun slowly rose out of the Caribbean Sea. Aldo got up from the bed and looked out the window. He could see the water in the distance. There were a few people gathered around a boat on the beach, probably fishermen, he thought. He felt a pain in his stomach and he hunched over. The reality of his situation hit him once more. He moved through the doorway into the adjoining room. It was the only other room in the cabin. It had a sink, a cupboard and a small table with two chairs. An old man was sitting at the table, eating from a bowl. He was small and wrinkled, very dark with grey dreadlocks. The man looked up from his breakfast. "G'day, mon," he said with a Rastafarian accent. "Did you sleep well?"

"Well, I did sleep a little, thank you," Aldo replied.

"Very good, mon, have some fruit, it will help you gain your strength." There were grapefruit and bananas on the table along with some sort of dried cereal. There were also two coconuts, one that had been split open. The man had some cereal in the bowl with coconut milk.

"It's OK," Aldo said, "I don't think my stomach could handle it." He held his hand on his stomach and grimaced as another cramp hit him.

"Oh, mon, you have a problem?" the old man said.

A big problem, one that's killing me, Aldo wanted to say. But, not to bother this man with his problems, he said. "My stomach's been upset for a while, probably just a virus."

The man thought about that for a minute, and said. "Let me help you." He got up from the table and went over to a cupboard. He opened it and took out what appeared to be an old jug. He came back to the table, took the lid off it and found an empty cup. He poured out about two ounces of a purplish liquid. It looked like a thick dark wine of some sort. He motioned to Aldo to drink it.

"What is it?" Aldo said.

"It is the juice of a berry bush that grows in the forest," he said. "It cures many illnesses. We have used it for centuries."

Aldo sniffed the cup. It smelled like fermented raspberries or a similar fruit. He thought it couldn't hurt and drank it down. He could feel it as it went down.

"Two times a day, mon," the man said, holding up two curled fingers. "It will be right here."

"Thanks," said Aldo, as he sat down at the table.

The two men talked for almost two hours. Aldo discovered much about these people he was with. They remained isolated because they were looked down upon by the other Rasta tribes on the Island because the others thought they had sided with the enemy when the British over took the island many years ago. Actually, they were compelled to help the British because they had stormed their village when they first landed on the island and took their women and children hostage. Even though they later made amends, the others on the island never trusted them. So, they kept to themselves on the far end of the island.

After a while, Aldo told the old man of his situation. The old man told him he could not understand about the insurance matters and chastised Aldo for trying to end his life. After chatting for a time, Aldo relaxed and felt more comfortable as the man seemed to take a genuine interest in his problems. He told Aldo he could stay there with him as long as he wanted. Aldo wondered just how long that might be.

CHAPTER TWELVE

Aldo spent the next few weeks resting and thinking about his situation. The people of the village accepted him, probably because of the old man who took him in. The man had said his name was Harry Potts and Aldo assumed he was an elder in the tribe and so whatever he approved, stood. He spent most of his days walking or sitting on the beach. Some of the village children became his friends, and he passed some time playing with them or telling them stories. Melky, became particularly close to him, and they spent many afternoons together. After attending the traps with his brother each morning, Melky went to a small school that was run by some of the village women. There, he learned basic reading and math, but the main focus was on teaching the history and culture of the tribe. After school, which ended around noon, Melky would head to the beach, where he would meet up with some of his friends and Aldo. They would play games, swim, or just sit and talk. These were the children he never had, Aldo thought, and he was enjoying them.

One afternoon, while sitting on the beach after a swim, some of the girls started braiding his hair, which had grown long. Soon, he had dreadlocks and, as the tropical sun browned his already dark skin, he was looking more and more like a native Rasta man. The children gave him a new name, Mensa, or wise one, because he helped them with their school work and told them stories, mostly fairy tales he had learned as a child.

Eduardo showed him how to use a blowgun, which the villagers sometimes used to hunt and fish. It was a bamboo type reed that one blew a sharp handmade dart through. They would set up coconuts about 20 yards away and try to hit them with the darts. Eduardo was pretty good at it, but Aldo needed more practice.

Some mornings, Aldo would go with the boys to check the traps. They would sometimes use the blowguns to shoot fish in the water. Although they weren't very successful, it was a fun game.

Aldo continued to take the berry concoction that the old man had given him, and although he figured it might just be his imagination, after a few weeks he actually started feeling better. The cramps and pain were easing and he was gaining strength. He thought about Angie all the time and wondered if he would ever see her again.

CHAPTER THIRTEEN

A ngie's life was at sort of a standstill. She got up, went to work, came home, wandered around her house and spent many hours thinking about Aldo. Would his body ever be found? Would their plot ever be discovered? Had he, in fact, perished in the Caribbean Sea? Could she ever be certain? She had George, but as his troubles deepened, she seemed to be losing him, too. He seemed to become more private, especially where the business was concerned. More drawers were locked, more files unavailable, and he made sure he saw the mail before she did.

One morning, when she arrived at the funeral home, there was an unfamiliar car sitting alone in the parking lot. When she got out of her car to open the office door, a burly looking man in a dark suit got out of his car and approached her.

"Hello, can I help you?" she asked as he came up to her.

"Is George in?" he said.

"No, I don't think so. He doesn't usually get here until nine," she said. "Can I help you?"

"No, I was trying to reach him. He seems to be avoiding me. He doesn't return my calls."

"What is this in reference to?" she asked.

"You're his girlfriend, ain't you?" the man said.

"Well, I'm his friend."

"You're his girlfriend and you can give him a message. Tell him Butch ain't too happy about the way he's been fulfilling his obligations, and the next time I got to come up here, it may not be such a cordial visit. You understand!" the man said, moving close to her.

"No, I don't understand, but I'll give him the message."

"Good, don't forget."

Butch walked back to his car and drove out of the lot. Angie tried to read the license number, but could only see that it was from New Jersey.

When George arrived she relayed the message, and showing concern, asked him what was going on.

"Well," he said. "Nothing really. I'm a little behind on the payments on the new furniture, but it's nothing to worry about. I'll call them today and straighten it out."

"George," Angie said. "Don't lie to me. That man sounded very serious and you haven't been yourself lately. What's going on? How bad is it? How can I help?"

George looked her in the eye. She didn't know it, but this is what he had been waiting to hear.

"No, you've done enough already. I'll work it out. It will take a while. But I'll be OK," he said, acting humble.

"George, I don't think that man will wait awhile, and you know I don't like to pry into your business affairs, but who else do you owe?"

"Oh, a few others. You know how slow it's been. Maybe I should sell out. But I don't know what I'd do."

"You couldn't do that. This place is your life. Why don't you sell your condo and move in with me?"

"Well, that would help my financial situation and I'm there most nights anyway, but I know how much you like your independence," he said sheepishly.

"Don't worry about my independence," she replied. "I want you to be safe."

"Well, thanks Ang. I'll think about it, but don't worry, things will work out."

"That's all right. It will still be my place and I will let you know who the boss is." She laughed.

"Listen," she said, "I will get you another check so you can pay these guys off. You don't need people threatening you. You can pay me back when you sell your place."

George had neglected to tell her that he had already refinanced his condo so many times to pay off previous gambling debts, that there was little equity left in it. But she didn't know this, and her generosity and caring demeanor made her an easy mark.

CHAPTER FOURTEEN

As the days turned to weeks, and perhaps months, Aldo began to lose track of time. He seemed to be getting stronger and his stomach problem was subsiding. He wondered if the berry juice he was drinking daily was actually some wonder drug that cured cancer. But whatever it was, it was helping him. His desire to get back to the real world was slowly overcoming his anxiety about being discovered and putting Angie at risk. He had to find out what had happened to her after he took his dive and disappeared.

After much thought, Aldo decided to venture out from the little corner of the world, which he would have considered paradise under different circumstances. When talking to the old man he found out the nearest major village or town was about a two-hour walk away. Shortly after dawn the next day, he left the village and started toward The Valley, the name of the town where he would start his exploration. It was the largest village on the island, in a valley surrounded by rolling hills and was designated as the capital. It was a hard walk because his shoes were an old pair of sneakers he had been given by one of the villagers, and there were no paved roads for the first half of the trip. But, it was a scenic hike as the path wound along the cliffs overlooking the coastline. He could see a few resort areas below. He tried to figure out if he was near the place where he and Angie had stayed. Nothing looked familiar, but as he walked, he found himself once again thinking of Angie. He thought about the last night he spent with her and how beautifully they had made love. His mind wandered back to the first time they were intimate so long ago.

It was the fall of 1970, the year he had graduated from UConn. He and Angie had become close friends throughout the two years after they had met, but, because of Angie's strict Catholic upbringing, had never consummated their friendship. This was frustrating for Aldo, because their best friends George and Freda were having sex on a regular basis and openly bragging about it. Angie had gone home to West Haven for the summer after Aldo graduated, and because he started a new job and career at IBM on Long Island, they had seen each other only a few times over the summer.

However, the annual fall UConn-Yale football game at the Yale Bowl in New Haven was an event they couldn't miss, and a perfect opportunity for the four of them to get together. Aldo and George reserved rooms at The Judges Cave Inn for the weekend, and they all met first thing Saturday morning.

After Bloody Marys and breakfast, they headed off to the Yale Bowl parking lot for some serious tailgating. Their group swelled to about 60 alumni and friends. They partied until game time and then went into the Bowl. When UConn scored, Aldo raised his leg to show his V for victory. After the game, they stayed in the parking lot until a police car pulled in and reminded them that the lot closed at dusk. They all decided to go downtown to The Toad, a college bar, where an upstart piano player that they knew from Hicksville, Long Island, was playing. By midnight they had had enough beer for one day. Aldo convinced Angie to stay with him that night, even though her home was 15 minutes away. She called her mother and told her she was staying with Freda for the night. They went back to the motel, tumbled into bed and made love for the first time. Before they went to sleep, Angie made Aldo promise to go to meet her parents the next day.

Sunday morning came and they eased their hangovers with more Bloodies and headed off to nearby West Haven. As they drove through New Haven, Angie had Aldo drive past Saint Mary's High School, the all girls Catholic school she had attended. They then drove down Wooster Street, and she pointed out where her father had grown up, and of course, Pepe's Apizza, the supposed originator of pizza pies in America. She explained how their family occasionally went there on Sundays when she was growing up. She promised Aldo she would bring him there before he went back to Long Island. When they got to West Haven, they drove past the cemetery where Angie's older brother, Joe, was buried. He had died a few years earlier in Viet Nam. Tears had come to her eyes as she recalled her closeness to her older brother. She had been in high school at the time. This was first time she had ever mentioned this to Aldo.

They then continued down Campbell Avenue to Savin Rock, an old amusement park along the beach. It was only two blocks from her home. She told Aldo how she and her friends would spend all their free time hanging out there. She told him how she worked at Jimmies Drive in as a busgirl during the summers when she was in high school. Aldo felt her enthusiasm and excitement as she recalled her childhood and adolescence. Her sense of family and friends impressed him, he now remembered. When they finally arrived at her family home, Angie's mom was preparing Sunday dinner and, of course, had set a place for the man they had heard so much about. They welcomed him with open arms like he was already a family member.

When they sat down to dinner, they feasted on antipasto, lasagna, meatballs and sausage. They drank homemade wine.

Aldo had barely enough room for the expresso and cannoli's, but he forced himself. After dinner, while the women cleaned up, Aldo and Angie's dad went out back to smoke cigars. It was mid-September and the late summer sun was warm and made jackets unnecessary. As they walked, Aldo noticed the grape vines that lined the large backyard. They were heavy with dark grapes ready for picking. Honeybees flitted about the vines searching for the last bit of nectar before the fall chill put an end to their work. The two men walked to a cleared area amidst the vines where a wooden picnic table and two wooden benches had been set up. Vitale Carini reached into his vest pocket and pulled out two long dark cigars. He picked up a small knife that was on the table and cut the tips off the two smokes. He handed one to Aldo and took a long wooden match out of his shirt pocket. He struck it on the table and offered Aldo a light. As Aldo put the cigar in his mouth and inhaled, the tip turned red and a puff of smoke rose skyward. Aldo felt the smoke in his lungs and a tightness in his chest. He let out a cough. Mr. Carini smiled.

When Aldo regained his composure they sat down at the table. They talked about football, the weather and Aldo's new job. It was then, on the spur of the moment, Aldo asked. "Do you think, I mean, would it be alright with you, if I asked Angie to marry me?"

Vitale Carini stared at him curiously, puffed on his cigar and said. "Well, I don't know. I don't even know you. Can you provide for her?"

"As I was saying, I just started a new job and the prospects for advancement look real good." Aldo paused. "And it wouldn't be right away. Maybe, at least a year. At least not until she graduates."

The old man took a long drag on his stogie, exhaled a puff of smoke and smiled.

"She speaks very good of you. She is my baby, you know, and if it makes her happy, I will give my blessing." He held out his hand and Aldo grabbed it enthusiastically.

"Please don't tell her for a while. I have to get some things in order first. I just wanted to clear it with you, so I can start planning," Aldo said.

"OK, son, we have omerta," he said as he gave Aldo a warm hug. Aldo smiled to himself, knowing from his own Italian upbringing that the word meant a code of silence.

Now, 28 years later, he remembered these events like it were yesterday. Mr. Carini had passed away soon after Angie and he were married.

As he walked along, Aldo thought about how he had fulfilled his promise to his father-in-law to provide for his daughter. He worked hard at his job at IBM and soon became head of his department. His annual salary provided him and his bride with a comfortable living.

Angie, with a degree in education, taught at a small private school in Oceanside, New York. At first, they rented a small apartment while they saved to buy a house. Eventually, they bought their present home in the upscale Muttontown section of Syosset. Over these years, their only problem seemed to be their inability to have children.

Then, Aldo recalled, in 1993 "Big Blue," as IBM was called, underwent some changes that would drastically affect the Ferraris' lives. The company was losing millions of dollars as the computer industry evolved and the pc and the internet became the driving force. When Louis Gerstner took over as CEO, he was determined to reverse the downslide and make the company profitable once again. Divisions were consolidated and departments eliminated, Aldo's included.

Aldo was offered another position, but it would be at the company headquarters, in Armonk, New York, quite a drive from Syosset. It was also at a lesser salary.

It was at that time that he and fellow employee, Jack Dorenz, decided to leave IBM and start their own consulting company. They lined up some major clients and opened D and F Consulting, offering software and programming services.

At the outset, the business thrived, and Aldo and Jack were very successful, soon making more money than either had at IBM. After some discussion, he convinced Angie to quit her job, since the money she was making put them in a higher tax bracket and netted them practically nothing. She could relax after 20 years of teaching , he told her, and she admitted that she liked that idea.

Aldo remembered now that that was not such a good idea, since his partner was letting their success go to his head. He had always been a heavy drinker, but now, with all the extra cash, he was a borderline alcoholic.

Jack began putting in less and less effort into his work. He would go on so called business trips to Las Vegas and other exotic spots, or just disappear for days at a time. He and Aldo argued constantly.

Aldo then recalled how it all came apart. At an important meeting with their top client, Jack showed up drunk and insulted the CEO. A month later, their contract was terminated. It was then that Aldo decided to end his relationship with Jack and split up the company. Much legal wrangling followed and one client after another left the fold.

Aldo had tried to start again on his own, but it was very difficult. He also sought employment elsewhere, but that too was one disappointment after another.

That also was when his medical problems started. He first thought it was from the stress of his company's misfortunes. He ate antacids like candy and gulped Maalox constantly. Finally, Angie convinced him to see a doctor. It was then that he found out that his former partner had let their health insurance lapse. This, along with his dire prognosis, had sent him over the edge, and he began planning his own demise.

Since he and Angie had been planning their anniversary vacation for some time, they decided to go ahead with it, even though he was unemployed and their savings were fast dwindling. That was also, he now remembered, when he decided when and how he would end it all. He now realized what a mistake that was.

CHAPTER FIFTEEN

As he got closer to his destination, Aldo passed by ramshackle homes, fields of goats and chickens, and then churches and small stores and one room cafés. As he approached the outlying areas of the town, the road became busier with pedestrian traffic, bicycles, mopeds and an occasional car or pickup truck. He looked like a native with his dark skin, dreadlocks and beat up wardrobe, and no one gave him a second look. He wandered into a sort of general store near the center of town and started looking around. He looked for a newspaper, but the only thing he found was a local monthly activities flier. He scanned through it and saw a listing for an event at the library. He thought this could be a place to get some information and maybe find a newspaper from the United States. He went to the counter and asked the clerk for directions to the library. He tried his best Rasta man accent and, though the clerk looked at him strangely, he told him it was three blocks down the next street, across from the police station.

Aldo went into the library not knowing what he would find or even what he was looking for. It was a very small building with about four rooms. The only people there were one older lady and the desk clerk. Aldo browsed around the book racks and went from room to room, opening one book and another. There was nothing he saw that could help him. Then, in the corner in the last room, there was something that made him do a double take. He looked again. There was a computer set up on a table and a sign which read, "Internet access- $5.00 EC- 1 hour limit." Aldo thought, "Could this be my access to the outside world?" He sat down and had barely put his fingers on the keyboard when the clerk came around the corner.

"You must pay in advance for the first hour," she said, in a demanding tone.

He realized that $5.00 EC was only about $3.00 in U.S. money, but he also realized that he had no money at all. He also knew he would probably need a lot of time to find the information he needed. These were two problems he would have to work out.

"Sorry, I forgot my money," he said as he got up. "I will have to come back."

As he was leaving, he noticed a sign near the entrance. "Janitor Needed-Part time-apply at desk." He turned and went back to the desk. The young woman was busy on her own computer when he approached. He stood there for a minute before she looked up. "Yes," she said.

"I am interested in the janitor job, if it is available."

"I think it is."

"What does it involve and what are the hours?" he asked.

"Just a minute." She opened a drawer in the desk and pulled out a sheet of paper. "It's right here," she said as she handed him the sheet.

He read over it quickly." 2 to 3 hours a night, 4 nights per week, after closing. Clean floors, bathroom, some windows, take out trash etc. $6 EC per hour."

"How do I apply?" Aldo asked.

"When can you start?" she asked.

"Anytime."

"How about tomorrow?"

"OK," he said, not knowing what he was getting into.

"Take this with you and fill it out. Bring it with you, around 4:00 p.m.," she said, as she handed him a form. "What's your name?"

"Mensa."

"OK, Mensa. See you tomorrow."

When Aldo left the library, he had some decisions to make. Should he go back to the village or try to find a place to stay here in The Valley? The information card the woman gave him asked for name, address, references, etc. What would he put down? How long would it take him to find what he was looking for on the web?

He decided to check out the town and then decide what to do. One thing he knew was that he was getting hungry, and he had no money.

He wandered down one street and up the next. He tried to remember the names of the streets. Many of the houses had no numbers, so he thought he could fake that part of the address on the form. He noticed many of the names on businesses were of English descent, because, he surmised, the island was a British Territory. Richardson, Hobbs, Cunningham, Rogers, Jones and Banks were the names he saw on various buildings. So, he decided his new name would be Jones, Mensa Jones. He spotted a deserted shack on Wallblake Street and decided his address would be North Wallblake Street. He was still hungry.

As he continued to wander the byways of The Valley, Aldo decided to go back to his village for the night. It was early afternoon and he could make it by nightfall. He would gather some basic items he would need, get a night's rest and come back in the morning. Then he would stay a few days until he got the information he was looking for, and then decide what to do.

On the way out of town, Aldo passed a market. He went in and when he thought no one was looking, he stuffed a piece of fruit into his shirt and left quickly. He felt bad about it. He hoped that his life had not come to being a homeless person, stealing food to survive.

CHAPTER SIXTEEN

George Macklin cashed the second $50,000 check from Angie and headed for Atlantic City. He had contacted Butch and arranged a place to meet him and pay off his debt. On the long ride down the New Jersey Turnpike, he toyed with the idea of hitting the casino first and trying to expand his bankroll. He also thought about how much he would actually have to give his creditor to keep him off his back for a while. Neither idea seemed like good financial strategy, but George never was good at money matters. He still owed $35,000 so that would leave him $15,000 to play with, he thought, not even thinking about his other debts or repaying Angie. He had thought about another plan, a devious one at that. He knew it could have serious consequences, deadly ones, but he decided to go with it.

After checking in, he went to the same bar where he and Butch had arranged their deal. Butch was waiting when he got there. George scanned the casino and lounge area as he walked, hoping perhaps he would see Gloria, but he did not.

"Mr. Macklin," Butch said, as George sat down. "Nice to see you. I'm glad you smartened up. I would have hated to cause any trouble for you in that nice, little town you live in."

"Yeah, sure. Thanks for your thoughtfulness. Johnny Walker Black on the rocks," he told the barmaid as she walked by.

"How much do you need?" George asked.

"Well, 20 grand will catch you up, but it would be nice if I didn't have to chase you around no more," Butch said sarcastically.

"I know, I got a little behind, but you didn't have to get nasty. I've always taken care of my markers before. Doesn't past history mean anything anymore?"

"Well, past history does, but your present and future history ain't looking too good," Butch retorted.

"So, how about I give you 25. Then maybe we can make a deal for the other ten. Give me an extra month or so," George offered, taking a long pull on his scotch.

"Sure, but that will cost you five more," Butch said.

George gulped. He thought that was not the deal he had come to make. "OK, come up to my room, I got the cash there. By the way, do you know a chick named Gloria?"

"I know a lot of chicks," Butch said, "No Gloria."

They left the bar together, went to the elevator and went up to the 12th floor. They talked about the Jets and Giants on the way, got off and went to George's room.

"Want a drink?" George asked.

"Nah, I'm really in a hurry," Butch said.

George had taken the precaution of putting the cash in the room safe this time, after his last experience. He went to the safe and retrieved the money. He counted out the $35,000 and handed it to Butch.

"I'm paying it all off. Can I get some kind of receipt for this?"

Butch smiled. "What, you don't trust me no more?"

"Well, I had a bad experience, and what if something happens to you before you get back to the office?"

"Boy, you are getting antsy with age," Butch said, pulling out a business card and scribbling something on it.

"Here, this will have to do, but if we can't do business on a handshake, maybe we shouldn't do business no more."

"Yeah, maybe we shouldn't," George answered.

"I'll be in touch," Butch said, as he put the cash in an envelope, tucked it in his jacket pocket and went out the door.

"I'm sure," George said, as he closed the door.

George knew he would be seeing Butch very soon, sooner than Butch expected. His plan was to get back some of the money he had lost to Gloria, since he was sure Butch and his friends had something to do with that story. He went to his night bag on the bed and pulled out a small brown case and a small plastic bag.

He waited a few minutes and then went quickly down four flights of stairs to the parking garage level. He waited around the corner and watched for the elevator to open. Sure enough, there came Butch.

George watched him as he went down the row of cars to his Lincoln Town Car. George moved quickly, bending low and darting between cars to avoid being seen by the security cameras positioned at the corners of the parking level. He took the case from his pocket as he walked and removed a small, very sharp, surgical knife which he used when preparing corpses for burial. He put on the surgical gloves he had in the bag.

When he arrived at Butch's car, he went alongside the driver's door and tapped on the window. Butch looked surprised, but when he recognized George he pushed the button to roll down the window. "What?" he asked.

George leaned in and quickly inserted the knife under Butch's chin. Moving it rapidly three inches from side to side, he severed Butch's windpipe and some arteries. Butch gasped as he began drowning in his own blood. He tried to get out of the car, but George held the door shut. Blood started oozing from Butch's mouth, and George reached behind and yanked his head back, further aggravating the mortal wounds.

Butch slumped back in the seat, as life left his body. George reached into the victim's jacket pocket and retrieved the envelope with the cash. He went into his other pocket and grabbed his wallet. He then quickly left the car and snuck back between the rows to the exit ramp. He ran up the ramp, staying close to the walls, again to avoid the cameras. When he reached the casino level, he removed the gloves and walked back into the hotel. He went immediately into the casino and to the lounge. It was only minutes after Butch's time of death and, if needed, George was establishing an alibi. He made sure he sat where a barmaid who recognized him would wait on him.

"The usual," George said. She brought him his Johnny Walker.

A strange calm came over George as the adrenaline rush left him. He had worked with dead people his whole life, but this was only the second time he had actually caused someone's death. Yes, his wife Freda's accidental drowning was far from accidental. The blow on her head wasn't caused by her falling. It caused her falling, right into the pool. George's mind wandered back as he now recalled how it happened.

CHAPTER SEVENTEEN

I t was over eight years ago and, as usual, he and Freda's relationship was in turmoil. He was never home, she was always drinking, and it had gotten really ugly when she suspected him of having an affair with a young widow whose husband George had just buried. She had confided in Angie that she was going to see a lawyer. Aldo had a talk with George and advised him that they should try to reconcile, go to counseling and persuade her to go to rehab for her drinking problem. They were old friends, and Angie and Aldo would do anything to help them stay together.

George had an easier solution, one where he wouldn't have to split his possessions 50/50 or pay alimony. Plus, he could collect on her life insurance.

That night George had gone to a Rotary meeting. It was over at 9:30 p.m., and he had gone to Sam's, a local bar three blocks from his home, to have a few drinks and discuss the meeting with some other Rotary members.

He had thought his plan over many times and waited for the opportunity to execute it. Freda liked to sip her martinis poolside whenever the weather permitted, and George knew she would be there tonight. At around 10:45, he excused himself and left for the men's room. He exited out the back door, cut through a parking lot and a few backyards and was in his own yard in seven minutes. Freda was dozing in her lounge chair by the pool. The pool was adjacent to the house and was surrounded by an eight- foot privacy fence. She would usually stay there until George came home. He would wake her, they would argue and she would stagger into the house and go to her own bedroom.

George went immediately to a tool shed near the pool. He found a small piece of concrete, the same material as the pool deck. He had saved it since the pool was installed a few years earlier. When hitting her with it, it would leave a residue on her skull, and appear as if she had fallen and hit her head. He called her name as he snuck up behind her. She slowly awoke and started to get up, just as he brought the block down on her head. She staggered and he shoved her. She toppled over off the edge into the deep end. She never struggled as she sunk to the bottom. She was dead weight. George watched her for a few minutes under the water in the iridescent pool lights. "Eerie," he thought, as she laid there on the bottom, face up. He tipped the cocktail table over, and the martini glass shattered so it looked as if she may have stumbled against it and knocked it over. He gave her one last look and retreated through the back yard. He still had the rock in his hand and carried it with him as he headed back to the bar. As he passed a sewer drain, he dropped it down the hole and continued on.

As he went in the back door of Sam's, one of his friends spotted him. "Where did you go?" he asked.

"The john was full. I really had to go, so I went outside."

"Oh," said the friend. "Well, we're leaving. See you later."

"OK," George said. "Have a good night." He went back to the bar, had another drink and then left. When he got home, he immediately called 911.

George had benefited financially from that deed also. As he now sat at the bar at Caesars, he felt the wad of bills in his pocket. He mused that there was one other person's death that could, if he played it right, be very beneficial, financially. He thought about Angela Ferrari.

CHAPTER EIGHTEEN

When Aldo got back to the village, he confided in the old man about where he had been and his new plans. The man understood Aldo's need to find out how his wife was faring without him, but could not understand how he would obtain the information from a machine at the library. And since Aldo couldn't help her anyway, what was the point of frustrating himself? But, he told him, he was always welcome to return.

"I have an old friend there in The Valley, Jimmy Barnes. He has a small store on East Shore Road. Maybe he can help you."

"Thanks, I'll look him up," Aldo answered.

The old man gave Aldo a supply of the berry juice to take with him in case he had a relapse of his stomach problem, which now rarely bothered him. Aldo wondered if he really had cancer that was in remission or he had been misdiagnosed. He told the old man he would return to visit him and the children as often as he could. The man told him to take the old bicycle he had to make his travels a little easier. Aldo hugged and thanked him and went to bed.

In the morning, Aldo arose with the sunrise and put his things together. He did not have much since he had arrived with nothing, but the villagers had been very generous in supplying him with the essentials. He met Melky and some children as they went to the school and explained that he was going away for a while, but would be back to see them. Melky took it hard and tears ran down his cheeks as he hugged him good-bye.

"Take me with you," Melky said, as he wiped away tears.

"I'd like to, but that wouldn't be fair to you or the others," Aldo replied. "Maybe, when I come back, you can come visit me a few days, we'll see." He said his good-byes and left.

At first, Aldo had to push the bike because the paths were so rocky, but once he reached a road he was able to make much better time. It was true about never forgetting how to ride a bike, he thought, as he rode along.

About 10:00 a.m. Aldo reached The Valley. That gave him a few hours to find a place to stay. He found the store on East Shore Road. It was a small house that used the two front rooms as a store. It sold everything from groceries to fishing gear to live chickens. Aldo parked his bike and went in. "Is Jimmy Barnes in?" he asked the woman at the old cash register. She was a tall dark woman wearing an old house dress, dirty beat up sneakers and a bandana tightly wrapped around her black curly hair.

"Who wants to know?" she asked, as she looked at him inquisitively.

"I'm Mensa Jones, and a friend of Harry Potts, who told me to look him up."

"Harry Potts, huh? Well you can tell Mr. Harry Potts that you can no longer look up Mr. Jimmy Barnes. You see, mon, Jimmy passed away six months ago."

"Oh, I'm sorry to hear that, I'll tell him," Aldo said.

"You do that. And what is that old mon doing these days? Still hiding down at Reef's End?"

"Yes, he's still there, doing fine, ma'am. Are you related to Jimmy?" Aldo asked.

"I was his fourth wife, until he died," she said. "How can I help you?"

"Well, I'm new in town, got a new job at the library. But I need a place to stay for a while, you know, until I get some money."

"Oh?" she said, scratching her chin. "There is a vacant room upstairs, not much, just a bed. I guess you can stay there."

"That's all I need. Thank you, if it will be all right."

"It will be all right as long as you don't make trouble or a mess of it. My boy over there will make sure you leave in a hurry if you do," she said, pointing to a rather large, rough looking young man, sitting in the corner, eating. He looked to be about 300 pounds, had long dirty dreadlocks and wore baggy overalls.

"Uh, yes, I see," Aldo said glancing over. "Can you show me the room?"

"Go around the back and up the stairs, mon, you can show yourself. And when you get paid it will be $5.00 a week. OK?"

"Fine," he said, moving back out the door.

"If you want food, it's $1 a day," she yelled at him as he left.

Aldo pushed his bike around the back of the house and went up the rickety stairs. He went into a small hallway that led to two small rooms. He looked in the first and noticed it was full of boxes and plastic bags. This can't be it, he thought and proceeded to the other room. It was tiny, with a small bed in the corner. It smelled very musty, but it had a window. He went in and put his sack of things down on the floor. He went to the window and tried to open it. It was stuck, but after a lot of nudging, it opened. A warm ocean breeze blew in and across the room. From the window he could see the sea in the distance. A room with a view, he thought, how nice.

Aldo could only guess what time it was from the sun's position, but he figured he'd better get to the library. Better early than late on your first day, he knew. He stopped back in the store and thanked the woman for the accommodations, and asked her for a pen. She got one, and he took out the application card for the job and filled it in with his new address, East Shore Road.

"Thanks," he said to her. "Whats your name?"

"Renata," she replied.

"Thanks, Renata, I'll, see you later."

CHAPTER NINETEEN

When Aldo arrived at the library, he saw that the time on the clock in front of the police station across the street said 3:10. He was a little early, so he sat out front until 3:30 and went in.

"Good afternoon, Mensa," the woman said from behind her glasses that hung on her nose. "Are you ready to begin?"

"Yes, good afternoon," he said, handing her the card.

She took it, looked it over and stuck it in a drawer. "Come with me." She led him down a hallway to a closet that she opened, revealing mops, brooms, cleaning solutions etc.

"Here are your supplies. If there is anything else you need, let me know and I will get it or send you over to Ashley's, where we have an account, OK?" she instructed.

"Sure."

"Now, you will need to sweep and mop the floors on a daily basis. Also, empty the trash baskets into the barrel in the rear of the building. Straighten up the chairs. Every so often I may have other projects such as the windows. I'll let you know. Oh, and the bathroom, of course. That's a pet peeve of the director. It must be spotless."

"Fine," said Aldo. "I'll do my best."

"When, you are done each night, write the time on this sheet, and leave out the rear door. Make sure it is locked behind you. Any questions?" she asked.

"No, I think I will be OK. Maybe something will come up and I'll ask you tomorrow."

"Good, I will be leaving shortly out the front door. Have a good night."

"You, too," Aldo said. "I'll see you tomorrow."

Aldo started going through the mops and brooms to see what he had. He walked around the halls thinking about where he would start and establish a daily routine. Of course, he couldn't take his mind off the computer in the side room and could not wait to get to it.

After about a half hour, he heard the librarian leave out the front door. He picked up the tempo of his cleaning and got everything done in another two hours. It looked pretty good, he thought. He noted the time on the sheet, and headed toward the computer in the front room. It was an older model Compaq Presario.

Aldo was very familiar with computers because of his years at IBM. He had worked in research and development developing new software for business applications. He had also worked on new security programs for networks and so he knew his way around website security.

He sat down and immediately got on the Web. Using Angie's user ID and password, which he remembered and hoped she hadn't changed, he was able to access Angie's email. His emotions got to him as he read her sent mail to her girlfriend Paula in Michigan. Tears fell from his eyes as he recalled his wife's face and features and loving ways. He had known that his feelings for her would overcome him when he started seeing familiarities again, but he figured to just let it happen and go on.

Angie's mailings told her friend she was surviving, getting by, but it would take her a long time to heal. Maybe never. When he read, "how much I miss Aldo," he broke down again. After a while, he got himself together and started exploring other areas. He went to the website of the local paper in Syosset and started looking in back issues for news of his death. Finding nothing, he went to the New York Daily News and then, after an hour of browsing, he found it on the New York Post website. Scanning the area news from around the time of his "accident", he came across what he was looking for.

"L.I. MAN DIES IN CARIBBEAN DROWNING ACCIDENT"

It was very strange reading his own death notice, but he had planned it this way. He wondered about the body that had been recovered because, for sure, it was not his.

He thought about George, and how he might have assisted Angie in carrying out the plan. And did it work? He figured he could find out easily enough. He accessed the Bank of Long Island website and tried to log on with his password. "Invalid Password" came on the screen. He figured she must have gotten rid of his bank ID's. He tried to remember her old password, hoping she hadn't changed that. He typed it in. Nothing! He tried again, changing a letter. No luck. After a number of tries using different combinations of letters, the site opened. He went to past activity and scrolled back a few months. There it was; A deposit of nearly $500,000. His plan had worked, he thought. She had followed it through. At first, he felt relief, but it quickly turned to despair when he realized he could never be Aldo Ferrari again without Angie going to jail for fraud.

They could never resume the life they once led or be together publicly. Why did he do this? Why didn't he seek a second opinion about his illness? It obviously could be cured. How could he face her? Would she ever forgive him?

Aldo needed a break. He would continue his investigations another night. He logged off the Internet and then went to Internet Explorer and, with a few more clicks, erased any trace of him being on line.

He turned off the lights and left through the rear door, making sure it was locked behind him. It was after midnight as he made his way along the deserted cobblestone streets. The moon was bright over the Caribbean, and there was a myriad of stars in the sky. The computer had helped him answer a number of important questions. He had discovered much information, but it also gave him much more to consider.

CHAPTER TWENTY

George had intended to take the money he had reacquired and start paying off some of the business obligations. After all, that was why Angie had lent him the money in the first place, so he could get back on his feet financially. But as he sat at the bar, trying to forget that he had committed another murder, the Scotch started to cloud his thinking, and the lure of the game took over. The thrill of winning or the agony of losing large sums of money was something he craved. After an hour and Five Johnny Walkers, the wad of cash in his pocket got to be too great a temptation, and he headed to the blackjack table. With all that cash and a brain clouded by Scotch, he played the high roller again, laying thousands on each hand. A crowd gathered around the table to watch his folly, as he quickly went through the bulk of his newly acquired windfall. When the dealer hit 21 one more time, he got up and pushed his way through the crowd. He stumbled to the elevator and back to his room, a broke and broken man.

When George awoke the next morning, the events of the night before hit him like a sledgehammer, pounding more fiercely than the affects the scotch were having on his head. He got his things together and left the room. When he got to the parking garage, he drove past the spot where he had disposed of Butch and to his surprise, the Lincoln Town car was still there. One could barely see that there was someone in the car, and George wondered just how long it would be until someone discovered his deadly deed. How long would it be, George thought, before either the police or Butch's employers, or both would come around asking about his and Butch's interactions on the night in question? He started going over in his head his responses to the questions he would surely be asked. As he left Atlantic City and headed up the Garden State Parkway, panic started to set in. By the time he reached the New Jersey Turnpike, he was already thinking seriously about an alibi and an escape route.

CHAPTER TWENTY-ONE

The moving van had brought George's belongings from his condo to Angie's house, and was just about to leave as George pulled into the driveway. Angie had the movers put mostly everything in the two rooms they had agreed George would occupy, and was writing them a check.

"Sorry, Ang," George said apologetically, as he came through the front door. "I got tied up at a meeting and hit a lot of traffic on the way back."

She stared at him, not knowing whether to believe him or not. "Well, I was getting nervous when I didn't hear from you last night or this morning. You could have called!" she said curtly.

"I know, again, I'm sorry. Did they bring everything?" he said, trying to change the subject.

"I guess everything you told them to. It's all in the back rooms," she said.

"Let me go check before they leave," he replied and went away. When he returned, he gave the drivers the OK, and they left. "Give me the invoice, Ang, and I'll get you a check on Monday."

"Here, sure," she said handing him the bill. "I know we talked about our individual freedoms in this relationship, George, but letting me worry like that is not fair."

"I know," he said, putting his arm around her. "I won't let it happen again, I promise you."

Angie was finding herself having stronger, personal feelings toward George lately and she wondered if this was something she should let herself do. She missed the bond she had with Aldo, and wondered if she could ever have that with anyone else. She had known George for as long as she knew Aldo, and they had always been like brother and sister. Now, that he was struggling, she felt a natural desire to help him, and this was triggering something else she hadn't felt before. She looked up into his eyes and he seemed truly remorseful. She felt she had got her point across.

"OK," she said. "Come on, let's get you settled."

They spent the rest of the day and night moving furniture, hanging curtains and arranging fixtures. Around 9:00, they broke out some wine and ordered takeout from a nearby Chinese restaurant. By the time the wine and food were gone, they were in the bedroom making up the bed, the last thing before calling it a night.

"Thanks a lot, Ang," George said, as he moved close to her as she slipped on the pillowcases.

"I had always hoped we would be this close someday, and I think Freda and Aldo would be happy for us too, don't you think?"

"Yes, we were a great foursome, and now there are two. Strange how things work out." She sighed. He moved closer, embraced her and let his lips fall on hers. Whether because of the wine or the moment, she let herself go and pushed her mouth more fully to his. They fell onto the bed and soon were naked under the sheets. Friends became lovers quickly, and when it was over, fell asleep in each other's arms, exhausted.

CHAPTER TWENTY-TWO

Angie had awakened early, looked over at George who was still asleep and wondered if she had done the right thing with him last night. She felt happiness when she thought of once again having an intimate partner, and guilt when she thought of Aldo. Not being able to sleep, she arose. She was making coffee when George came into the kitchen. They looked at each other and each smiled wryly. He came over and gave her a kiss on the cheek.

"Good morning. Boy, I had this wonderful dream last night and you were in it," he quipped.

"Are you sure it wasn't a nightmare?" she shot back.

"No, it was beautiful, and I hope there will be more like it."

"Don't count on it, unless you plan on buying a lot of wine," she joked.

George poured himself a cup of coffee and said, "As I was saying last night, before we were interrupted by our passion, thanks for all you've done. I hope I can repay at least the companionship and love you've given me."

She thought about what he said and then replied, "We'll see. I think this may work out for both of us. George, you see, I think I need someone, too."

"Good!" George answered as he thought to himself how it all was working out perfectly.

CHAPTER TWENTY-THREE

Aldo arrived back at East Shore Road after his first night at the library. He went into the store through the rear door. Because it was late, there was no one around. He was very hungry so he grabbed himself some snacks and wrote an IOU for a dollar, left it on the register and went upstairs. He was exhausted from his long day and long trip. He became even more exhausted as the information he had acquired sunk into his brain. He now knew that Angie had followed his plan and collected the insurance money. How she did so without his body was still a mystery to him. He knew she was still suffering his loss, but wondered how could he, from where he was now, help her. He fell asleep and dreamt of her soft body next to him. He was with her once again, comforted by her love and affection, her caring touch, her warm smile.

Aldo awoke abruptly when something or someone, came suddenly between them. It seemed to be something dark, something dangerous, and something deadly. He sat up in bed, shaking. He got up and went to the window. He gazed out at the moon, shining on the sea. He had an ominous feeling that Angie was in trouble and needed help. He knew he had to somehow get back to her.

CHAPTER TWENTY-FOUR

It was Sunday morning, but George said he had an appointment at the home with relatives of a recently deceased man. He left, and Angie puttered around, rearranging furniture and moving things here and there. After all, there was a man in the house once again.

She was still having mixed feelings about the night before. Aldo wasn't even gone a year and she was making love to another man. Yet, she had someone to care for again.

Angie decided to do laundry, and went to George's bathroom to get his towels. As she went into his bedroom, she noticed his overnight duffel bag on the floor, and thought he must have some laundry in there that she could do, also. She unzipped the bag and saw a plastic hotel laundry bag with some clothes sticking out. She pulled them out, and as she did so, she noticed the small brown case. She picked it up and curiously opened it. She saw the knife, and after stopping to wonder, she thought, "Well, he was at a mortician's conference, so maybe he purchased it from a vender." It did look like it had been used, because there appeared to be tiny specks of blood on the handle, but she figured it was just her imagination, and she closed the case and put it back where she found it.

She took the bag of dirty clothes and went to the laundry room area next to the kitchen. She pulled out George's blue Oxford shirt, a pair of socks, a T-shirt and some briefs. She was about to discard the bag when she noticed something else in the bottom. She reached in and quickly drew back her hand. In the bag were two bloodied, latex gloves. She was startled at first, but then thought that maybe he was involved in a demonstration of some sort at the conference. But why would he bring the gloves home? She quickly stuffed the laundry items back in the bag and returned them to the duffel bag. "I'll let him bring it up," she thought, as she left the room confused.

In the next few days the gloves and knife were not discussed. She didn't know how to approach the subject without seeming suspicious, and he seemed to avoid any discussion of where he had been or what he had done over the weekend.

On Wednesday, as Angie arrived at the funeral home, she noticed a strange car in the lot again. It was a different car, but with New Jersey plates. It was a dark sedan with an extra antenna on the trunk. "Maybe a police car?" she asked herself. The door to George's office was ajar and as she walked by, she stopped where she couldn't be seen and tried to listen.

Inside detectives Sgt. Sean O'Byrne and Sgt. Sal Diglio of the Atlantic City Police force introduced themselves and were questioning George about his whereabouts on Friday past.

"Do you know this man?" O'Byrne asked as he showed George a picture of Butch Rogers.

"Yes," George said. "He's an old high school buddy I see on occasion in Atlantic City."

"When was the last time you saw him?" Diglio asked.

"Uh, just the other night, I guess it was Friday. I ran into him at the bar at Caesars. Why, what's the matter?"

"He was found dead in his car in the parking garage on Saturday morning. Somebody slit his throat," O'Byrne stated.

In the hallway outside the door, Angie gasped. She regained her composure and leaned closer to listen more intently.

"Oh, my God!" she heard George reply. "He was a real nice guy. Who would do that?"

"Well, it could have been robbery. His wallet was missing," Sgt. Diglio explained. "But, as you probably know, he had some shady connections. There's a rumor he was withholding some of his so called collections from his bosses. Did he give you any indication he was in trouble?"

"No, we just chatted for a few minutes. I didn't notice anything different about him," George replied.

"Why did you meet him? Did you owe him money?" O'Byrne asked.

"No, it was just by chance. Like I said, I knew him from high school."

"About what time did you see him last?" Diglio asked.

"Let's see," George mused, "I think it was around 9:30, maybe 9:45."

"What did you do after that?" said O'Byrne.

"I went to the tables. I didn't have a good night."

"We know, you lost quite a bundle," stated Diglio.

"Yeah, I guess that information is always available to you folks."

"Well, you must know, casino security have eyes everywhere," George felt uneasy but managed to not show his emotions.

The detectives stirred in their chairs and Angie, thinking they were about to leave, moved to her desk. A few minutes later, as George escorted the officers out, Angie heard them say. "So, Mr. Macklin, this investigation will be continuing, and as long as you keep yourself available, and are cooperative, there will be no need for a subpoena."

"I certainly will," George replied courteously." I am just as anxious as you to find out what happened to Butch. Like I said, he was a real nice guy."

They left, and George went back to his office, walking past Angie without saying a word.

When the officers were gone. Angie got up and went to George's office. The door was closed but she walked right in. George was at the window, staring out. "Who were those men?" she asked.

George turned around slowly. He was reluctant to discuss this with her, but he knew she had seen them, and would not let it rest.

"They were cops from Atlantic City. A fellow I saw there the other night was murdered, right after I saw him."

"Wow, what do they think happened?" she asked, acting surprised.

"He was involved with the mob. They think he might have stolen money from them."

"How was he killed?" Angie persisted.

"I guess they slit his throat, left him in his car in the parking garage."

The thoughts of the knife and gloves in George's bag immediately ran through her mind. She paused for a moment and steadied herself. "Ooh, that's awful," she murmured. "Were you able to help them?"

"Well, I told them what I knew, but I really couldn't help them too much."

She paused again, and then asked, "George, what's going on? How much were you involved with this guy?"

"I told you," he shot back, "or I told them, I only saw him a few minutes, that's all. I have no idea what happened to him. I feel bad about what happened, but he was in with a rough crowd, and I guess he ended up paying for it."

"Well, maybe you should stay away from that place, too."

"I was there on business. The meeting was two blocks away. I always stay there. I get my room for free."

"You wouldn't get your room for free if you weren't there gambling so much," she said sternly.

"Well that's my business. Don't you have work to do?"

Angie turned around and walked back to her desk, trying to shake off the terrible thoughts in her head. George walked past her toward the front door. "I've got to go out. See you at home." Angie stared out the window in silence.

CHAPTER TWENTY-FIVE

At a table in the far corner of the barroom at Tata's Supper Club on East Washington Street in Lodi, New Jersey, two men, Mikey "the shark" Barbierio and Rosario DeLuca, sat discussing the demise of their associate, Butch Rogers, the night before. They sipped Sambucco Romano with their coffees, and puffed on dark cigars. Close by, Stephanie, also known as Gloria, DiNuzzo, sat at the bar, reading the Enquirer. The men spoke softly to each other and then the older one said, "Dinuzz, come over here."

Stephanie slid off her stool and walked over.

"Sit down a minute," said Mikey.

Mikey was a dapper, well-dressed man in his mid-70s. He was born and raised in Brooklyn by his immigrant parents from Palermo, Italy. He owned Tata's and ran his other "businesses" out of there. "I'm really sorry about Butch," Stephanie said as she slid into the circular booth.

"Yeah, we all are," Mikey replied. "You know, we don't usually like to screw over our clients, but this Macklin guy fucked over my friend Geno over on Long Island, and I was just returning a favor when I had you grab his cash. Do you think this Macklin guy knew about you and Butch, that you guys set him up?"

"I don't think so. Me and Butch never even got close to each other that night, but, you never know. He had to be real pissed off at me."

"Did you ever see him again?" Mikey asked.

"No, I ain't been back there since, but my friend, Carole, the cashier, said the security guy was asking about me the next day. So, who knows?"

"Ok, get lost," Mikey said.

"You have a nice day, too," DiNuzzo said sarcastically, as she walked back to the bar.

"I think this guy had to do him," the shark surmised. "He was there last night. He is a coroner, see, and knows how to use a blade. He was up to his balls in hock, and besides, he stills owes us big."

"Well, what do you want to do?" asked Rosario.

"We got to set an example. We can't let this stand. It will hurt our reputation, you know what I mean?"

"Sure, we'll pay him a visit."

"Take him out, Butch was like family."

"Ok, boss, done!"

CHAPTER TWENTY-SIX

At his second day of work at the library, Aldo had discovered more information about Angie. Going back to his bank's website, he found that his wife had made two $50,000 withdrawals from her savings account, both checks written to George Macklin. From her emails to her friend he knew that George had moved in with her. He wondered what was going on. George was his best friend, and he and Angie had always been close, he thought like brother and sister. Maybe George felt he had to take care of her, now that her husband, his best friend, had died. But, Aldo thought, "Wasn't she taking care of him, giving him $100,000." He had another sleepless night. He wondered what would happen if he contacted her via email. Would he set her world upside down if she had decided he was gone and was making a new life with George? What if he contacted George and let him know he was still alive, and not to make any permanent plans with Angie? Would George keep the secret until they figured a way to bring him back without losing the insurance money, or going to jail?

Aldo knew he had to do something. It would drive him crazy to just stay here. He loved his wife too much to know she was with someone else, even his friend, George. And from what seemed to be happening and from the little information he had, George was starting to control her, just like he had done his wife, Freda.

Aldo always thought that Freda drank because she found herself trapped in a relationship with a very controlling, egotistical man. He remembered that after Freda died, George spent little time grieving, and at times even seemed relieved that she was gone. He saw it when he and George were together without Angie. He never mentioned it to her, because he knew how close she and Freda were. The more Aldo thought about this, the more worried he became. He knew he had to act. He began to formulate a plan.

CHAPTER TWENTY-SEVEN

It was a warm early spring day on Long Island. The sun was shining brightly, lawns were starting to turn green, and flowers buds were beginning to bloom. It was the kind of day that would make one feel happy, think good thoughts and be glad to be alive. George Macklin felt none of these things. He had just had a phone conservation with one of Butch's associates who not only emphasized that George still owed him $35,000 plus but also said he knew who killed Butch, and someone would be held accountable. George told him that he had a receipt for the money he had repaid, and the man just laughed. The Atlantic City detectives had paid him another visit and said they were reviewing the hotel security tapes from that night. They were trying to clarify the image of a man seen running down the parking garage ramp.

George's relationship with Angie was not going well, either. Since their argument after the detectives' first visit, she had become rather distant, only talking to him when she had to.

George stopped at the Syosset Post Office on his way to pick up some lunch. He got the funeral home mail out of the box, and as he was leaving he noticed there was a letter in his second box, the one he kept for his personal mail that he did not want to come to his home or the office. Only a few people knew about it, and he checked it rarely. He searched for the key in a pocket of his wallet and opened the little door. He took out the letter, and stared at the return address. "The Valley Public Library, Anguilla, B.W.I."

"What could this be? Why was it mailed to this P.O. box number?" he wondered. It must be a mistake, he thought, as he walked back to his car. He sat in the car and opened the envelope. It was a letter requesting donations to the library fund, but on the back was a hand written note. It read:

"George, This may or may not come as a surprise to you, but I did not die when I went over the edge. I am alive and living under cover on the island. I can't contact Angie for fear of having the insurance money revoked, or worse, having her arrested for fraud. I remembered the mail box number you told me about. Please take care of her until I can get enough money to come back to the States and work this out. Don't tell anyone, especially her, that you heard from me. I will be in touch soon about when I will be coming back. Just in case you might think this is a hoax, the V on my ankle is for victory. Thanks, buddy, Aldo."

"Holy shit!" George thought, as he reread the note. "This is all I need now. He comes back and the plot is found out and I'm one who will pay, too. I signed the papers, and I cremated the wrong body."

As he sat in his car, beads of sweat forming on his brow, George's heart and mind were racing as he tried to determine what he should do. He knew he had to get away. The mob and the police were after him, and now he had another problem, Aldo. He ran through one plan after another and then decided his best solution was to go to Anguilla and try to find Aldo. If he could persuade Angie to go, he thought he might be able to get rid of two problems at once, kill two birds with one stone, so to speak. He would also be thousands of miles away from the mob and the police. This, he thought, was his best way out.

CHAPTER TWENTY-EIGHT

Later that night, Angie was at home in her kitchen, preparing dinner, when George arrived. She was still unsure of her relationship with him, and she had more or less avoided him since their latest confrontation.

George came in to the kitchen, puttered around a bit and finally approached her. "I know we haven't been on the best of terms lately, but we've got to talk," he said hesitantly.

"OK, talk," she answered curtly.

"I just found out on a Caribbean website that they are holding two unidentified bodies in the morgue on Anguilla. I know it's been a while, but are you still interested in finding Aldo's remains?"

"Of course, if there is a possibility, I would certainly want to follow it up. Didn't we discuss this before?" she answered.

"Well, it is a possibility. I spoke to an official at the morgue, and from what he could tell me, it could be him. And they will only hold the bodies for another seven days, and then they will be buried."

Angie walked over to the window and stared out, in serious thought. She turned back to George. "When can you go, George, I can try to book your flight right away."

"I was hoping you could go, too. You wouldn't want to show up at the morgue, of course, but you could help me get the paperwork in order, if it is Aldo's body. Plus, we both could use a little R and R away from here, don't you think?"

Angie did not want to spend three or four days together with George anywhere, but this was something she thought she had to do. She busied herself around the kitchen, thinking over his proposition, and finally said, "All right. I'll try to get us a flight as soon as possible."

"Leave the return open, in case it takes us longer than expected," he said, "Let's hope we can put some closure on this and get on with our lives."

"Let's hope so," Angie thought, but she had serious doubts.

CHAPTER TWENTY-NINE

Aldo stared at the screen in front of him in disbelief at what he was reading. As usual, it was late at night and he was on the library computer checking on Angie's recent activities. He had opened an e-mail to Angela Ferrari from American Airlines, confirming her flight reservations to Anguilla via San Juan for Wednesday, Flight 832, Departing JFK at 8:15 a.m., and arriving at Wallblake Airport, Anguilla, BWI at 4:10 p.m., two passengers, Angela Ferrari and George Macklin.

"What! Why would they be coming here?" he wondered out loud. "Had George told her about his letter? Hadn't he asked him not to? What was he up to now? Are they coming to try to find him? Should he hide or be there to greet them?"

Aldo checked Angie's bank account. There was another large withdrawal. What was going on? He logged off the computer, locked the library and left. He got on the used motorbike that he had just purchased with some money he had saved from his job and rode home. It was Tuesday, and he had only one day to contemplate what he should do before his wife and friend showed up on the island. As he climbed the back steps, he noticed a light was on in his room. He thought he didn't leave it on, but maybe he could have. When he opened the door, he was shocked to see the two boys, Eduardo and Melky, sitting on his bed.

"What are you guys doing here?" he asked.

"Um, ah, hi Mensa," Eduardo stammered.

"We ran away!" Melky exclaimed.

"Ran away? Why, how long have you been here?"

"We had an accident. We lost the boat. They will be really mad at us," Eduardo explained.

"We had a hard time finding you. We knew you would help us, won't you, Mensa?" Melky asked.

"I don't know. What happened?"

The boys explained that they had raced their boat against another group of boys. They then crashed on some rocks, running away after the other boys chased them for not paying off their bet. Then they decided to escape and find Aldo. Eduardo asked him if they could stay there for a few days, until they could figure out what to do.

"You have got to let your parents know where you are. They will be worried sick," Aldo said.

"Momma and Papa went to St. Maarten. We were staying with our friends. They must think we went home."

"Are you sure? You wouldn't lie to me, now, would you?"

"No, no, Mensa. We are telling the truth," sobbed Melky.

"Well, we will all go back first thing in the morning and get this straightened out. You can stay here tonight, but no longer, OK?"

"OK," Melky said.

"OK, thanks," Eduardo chimed in.

This was a distraction Aldo did not need at this time, but he loved these kids, and he thought he could get them home and still be back by the time Flight 832 arrived at Wallblake. After talking for a while, the boys fell asleep. Aldo's mind went immediately back to Angie and George. He slept very little that night.

CHAPTER THIRTY

Angie had gone to bed early in anticipation of her next day trip. As she lay in bed, trying unsuccessfully to fall asleep, she wondered what she was getting herself into. She had grown more and more suspicious of George and his recent doings, the police, the knife, the hoods looking for him. And yet, here she was going away with him to discover who knows what? And besides this, she was going back to which a place where she had lost her husband, to find his body, which she had already buried. She turned over again and hugged her pillow. Perhaps she shouldn't go. No, she would not, she decided. She would tell George in the morning that she had changed her mind, that she did not feel up to it.

George also had a lot on his mind, as he packed his overnight bag for their early morning flight. He had gotten rid of the knife and gloves, and now was packing another little surprise. In the drug cabinet at his mortuary he had found the bottle of gamma hydroxyl butyrate, (GHB), a very strong sedative, which he had saved from the days when he was planning Freda's demise. It was a knockout drug, which most recently became notable in date rape cases. With the right timing, it could render Angie senseless, while he took her to the place where Aldo had died. Under sedation, he felt he could convince her to go join Aldo, after writing a suicide note explaining she could no longer go on without him. He had already drawn up the note. He knew, in the stupor she would be in, he could persuade her to and sign it. He would then find Aldo and dispose of him. His good friends, the Ferrari's, would be together at last. He would then disappear somewhere in the Caribbean until things cooled down, and then return to the states to retrieve the proceeds from Angie's estate.

George was about to retire for the night when he heard a noise at the front door. He looked out the window and saw two men standing next to a car at the end of the driveway. The front door rattled again. "Shit, someone's trying to break in!" he said out loud. As he came out of his room, Angie was coming down the hall.

"George, what's that noise? What's going on?"

"We've got to get out of here!"

"Why?"

The front door banged open. "Someone's after us, that's why! Get your bag! Don't ask questions! I'll explain later."

"Call the police!!" Angie screamed.

"We can't. Let's go, Now!!"

George grabbed the bag they had packed for the trip. He led Angie quickly through the kitchen and down the backstairs into the garage, which was under the raised ranch house. They could hear voices shouting upstairs. They threw their bags in the backseat of the car and jumped in. George started the car and pushed the garage door opener remote on the visor. The door started up. As soon as it was opened far enough, George gunned the car down the driveway. The two men near the other car appeared shocked as the car sped toward them. One drew a gun from his coat and pointed it at the car racing toward him. Just before hitting the car blocking the driveway, George veered left, going across the lawn and through the hedges. A bullet ricocheted off the trunk.

"Stay down!" George shouted at Angie, pushing her onto the floor. She was sobbing uncontrollably. Once in the street, he turned right, hit the accelerator and sped away. The men jumped in their car and came after them. At first, they were right behind George's car, but they didn't know the streets like George did. They were moving extremely fast for city streets, as George swerved past other cars.

As they headed south on Jericho Turnpike, a tractor trailer came at them from the other direction. Just as it got to them, George veered left in front of the truck. The driver jammed the brakes and the truck jackknifed across the road. The pursuers hit the brakes to avoid the truck and skidded right, sideswiping three parked cars before stopping, as George and Angie sped away down a side street. After a few quick turns, they were on the Long Island Expressway. Once on it, and George felt assured they were no longer being followed, he slowed down. As they got close to JFK they exited the highway, and found a motel to hide out for the night.

Angie, speechless all the way, finally spoke, "George, I can't do this. What have you got yourself into? Why were those men after us, shooting at us, trying to kill us? Who are they?"

"It's a long story," he replied. "I borrowed some money from the wrong people, all right! I'm sorry you had to get involved. But we will get away to the island tomorrow, and I'll try to straighten it out before we come back. We'll be safe there. I'll call the police, I promise. Please stick with me, Ang, we'll be OK."

"Borrowed money?" she asked. "I gave you money. I could give you more. Why did you have to go to them?"

"I know. But I thought you helped enough. I didn't want to ask for more. I'm sorry." He tried to put his arms around her, but she pulled away.

"I'm just so confused," she said "I don't want to go anywhere tomorrow. I need time to think."

"They will find you," he pleaded. "They will try to hurt me by hurting you. Anguilla is the safest place right now. We'll be out of here first thing in the morning. When we get there, you can get your own place. Be alone, if you wish. Trust me on this.

"I don't know if I can anymore," she said.

CHAPTER THIRTY-ONE

A few hours later, George and Angie left the motel, and drove to the airport. George dropped her off at the curbside check-in and went to park the car. She was nervous and kept looking around her. Many black limos and town cars, like the one in her driveway last night, were in the drop-off area, and she eyed each one suspiciously. One pulled slowly by as the clerk was checking her bag, stopped for a second, and then pulled over and double-parked. Two men got out of the car and started toward her. She took her receipt and quickly moved inside the terminal. The men followed in quick pursuit. She hurried down the concourse as they narrowed the distance between her and them. As she rounded a corner, she spotted a ladies' rest room and ducked in. She went quickly into a stall, and waited nervously for ten minutes. She knew she couldn't stay there forever, and wondered if the men would be waiting outside when she left. As she came out of the stall, a woman security guard in uniform was washing her hands in a basin.

"Excuse me," Angie blurted. "Could you tell me where Gate 12 is?"

"Sure," the woman said, turning toward her. "It's just down the way, left out of here, but you will have to go through a security checkpoint."

"Are you going that way? I get lost easily," Angie asked.

"Sure, come on, I'll show you."

As they left the ladies' room, Angie spied the two thugs waiting across the way. She stuck very close to her escort as they made their way down the concourse to the security checkpoint. The men followed close behind. There was only a small line, and Angie showed her boarding pass and slid right in behind the barriers. She thanked the woman who helped her, and moved close to her next friends, the agents at the checkpoint. She put her purse and jacket on the belt and went through the detector with no problems. She finally felt safe because her pursuers had no boarding passes, and were stopped at the checkpoint. She waited for George.

Angie could see the men standing on the side of the hallway when she spotted George coming down the concourse. The men would surely grab him, she thought, if they saw him. As one of the men looked at her across the barriers, Angie raised her hand in front of her face and rolled all her fingers down except for the middle one, making an obviously obscene gesture at them. The one who saw her poked the other, visibly annoyed as Angie mouthed the words, "F you, Asshole" at them. They grew angrier at her and raised their fists and were distracted as George snuck by them unnoticed. When he saw her, she pointed to the men, and he quickly pushed into the line at the checkpoint. It was too late for the thugs to do anything, and they walked away angrily.

When George got through the detectors, he joined her and she hugged him. "Were those the men from last night? They chased me," she asked, pointing at the two retreating toward the exits.

"I don't know. I suppose they were. They must have found out our itinerary somehow. We're OK now," George mumbled.

"Sure, if they don't follow us to Anguilla," Angie sighed.

They boarded the plane and Angie was able to relax as the plane climbed over the city and turned out over the Atlantic, not realizing that her worst enemy was sitting next to her.

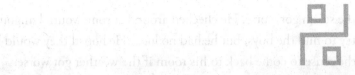

CHAPTER THIRTY-TWO

Aldo arose early on Wednesday morning after a sleepless night. He had decided not to contact his wife and friend when they first arrived. Instead he would try to follow them, and try to figure out why they came here at this time. He knew he could keep fairly close without being recognized, because of his dreadlocks, deep tan and native appearance. At the appropriate time, he thought, he could make himself known, and reunite with Angie.

The boys had gone downstairs to the store to get some breakfast. Aldo told them to put it on his account, and that he would be right down, and they could then leave and return to their home in the village.

When Aldo went into the store, the boys were nowhere around. He asked about them, and Renata told him that they had picked up some snacks and rode off on their bicycles. Aldo ran out, but they were nowhere in sight.

He really wanted to wish them good-bye and make plans to see them again, and he didn't have time to chase them. He got on his scooter and went into town.

The weather on the island had become quite windy, and people were talking about a tropical storm that was brewing and possibly headed toward them. He went by the library to say he would not be in that night, and the clerk said they would probably close early if the storm got worse. He checked around at some youth hangouts to try to find the boys, but he had no luck. He hoped they would have the sense to come back to his room if the weather got worse.

Aldo went over to the airport and checked the incoming flight schedule and found out that most flights out of San Juan were experiencing delays. Flight 832 was now due at 5:30 p.m. On his way back to town, it started raining, and the wind began picking up. By noon, it was clear that the storm could pass over the island. It was not yet a hurricane, but store owners and home owners began making preparations, in case it got worse. Aldo made a last check around town for the boys, and then headed back to the airport.

CHAPTER THIRTY-THREE

In San Juan, George was making last minute preparations to make sure his trip was a success. He left Angie at a coffee shop in the terminal and went to a phone and called an old acquaintance. Rico Fuentes was a native-born Puerto Rican who had spent some time in the States, before fleeing back to his homeland. George had buried Rico's friend after he was killed in a drug deal gone bad. He still owed George money. Before he left, George was able to obtain his phone number from a friend in New Jersey. Rico picked up the phone at his uncle's store in San Juan.

"Rico?" George asked.

"Who's calling?" Rico answered in a disguised voice.

"George Macklin, your friendly undertaker," George quipped. "Your mama asked me to call you to see how you were."

"Oh, George, I'm OK. Where are you?" a surprised Rico asked.

"Well, I'm here in San Juan, and I need a favor. If you can help me, I can forget what you owe me and even tell mama you paid me back and are doing fine."

There was a long pause. "Mama? You talked to her?"

"Sure," George lied. "She was wondering how you were doing and said to call you if I needed a favor."

After another wait Rico said suspiciously, "What can I do to help you?"

"Well, here's my story," George continued. "I'm on my way to Anguilla. You know anyone there who could hook me up with a piece. You know, a gun. I'm in a little trouble and I might need something for protection, you know what I mean?"

After another pause, Rico said, "Ok, yeah, I know a guy over there, Martin Alvarez. He drives a cab. I'll call him. Call me back in 15 minutes."

"Good," said George. "You're a good man, Rico."

George waited and then called Rico back after 15 minutes had passed. Rico told him that Martin Alvarez would meet him at the cab stand at the airport, and get him what he needed.

After George hung up, Rico immediately placed a call to Lodi, New Jersey, to talk to someone he owed a bigger favor than the one he owed George.

The bartender at Tata's put Mikey on the phone and he and Rico had a conversation that put George and Angie in serious danger.

CHAPTER THIRTY-FOUR

Wallblake Airport was a small island airport with three runways and a small terminal. It handled only small prop planes from other major Caribbean ports of call. Passengers boarded and departed their planes on the tarmac and walked to the terminal. At 6:00 p.m., passengers from Flight 832 started coming off the tarmac and through the arrival gate. It was raining and there was a strong wind, and the passengers hustled to get inside quickly.

Aldo was sitting in the rear of the reception area with a newspaper over his face. With his new looks, his friends would never recognize him, he thought, but he covered up anyway. When he spotted Angie his heart started to race, and he almost jumped from the spot where he was sitting to run to her. He had a hard time containing himself, but he did and melted as she walked by him. George and Angie claimed their bags and proceeded through customs. George went to the cab station while Angie waited. Martin Alvarez was waiting for them next to his cab. He looked like a typical islander, about 30 years old with a dark complexion, a pencil-thin moustache and black curly hair under a baseball cap. He was wearing cut off jeans and a faded floral shirt. When he spotted George, he approached and introduced himself. George then motioned to Angie that this was their ride. Aldo watched closely as they put their bags in Mr. Alvarez's cab and got in. He went to his moped and moved close enough to follow them as they left the airport grounds. Because the roads on the island were narrow and bumpy, vehicles had to proceed slowly and it was easy for Aldo to follow. They went directly to Shoal Bay and a small resort hotel called The Allamar Beach Club. There was a main building with two floors of suites surrounding a pool area, and two other one-story buildings with one-room cabanas. There was a small restaurant adjacent to the pool. It was a short walk to the beach and about a quarter mile along the beach to the beach house Angie and Aldo had rented for their vacation over a year ago. George paid the cabbie and then when Angie started toward the hotel entrance, asked him quietly if he had spoken to Rico about the gun.

"Yeah, mon," Martin said. "I am gettin it for ya tonight. Meet me down on the beach in the morning at dawn, at five. I will have it."

"OK, good. I'll be there. I'll take care of you," George said as he shook Alvarez' hand.

After checking in, George suggested to Angie that they should get something to eat, and a nights rest before they went to the morgue and reviewed the bodies, especially after their last night's adventure.

Aldo had parked his bike, and was out of sight among the ferns and palm trees, while George and Angie checked in. When they came around the side to their room, he followed, sticking close to the building. He could see the door to their room, on the first level, from where he was. It was across the courtyard, near the cabanas adjacent to the pool. Soon after, they emerged and went to the restaurant.

The restaurant was in a small building, adjacent to the pool, also. It was decorated with large ferns and tiki lights, and Caribbean artwork on the walls. There were only six tables, and there was only one other couple in the restaurant. A native hostess brought them menus.

Angie was still too upset to eat, and only ordered a salad. George ordered an appetizer and a bottle of wine. They planned what they would do the next day and both agreed, whatever the outcome, it would not be pleasant. When Angie dismissed herself to go to the ladies room, George removed the vial from his pocket and deposited a few drops in Angie's wineglass. He refilled it, and poured the rest of the wine into his own glass. When Angie returned, they finished, signed the tab and walked back to their room. As soon as the hotel room door closed, Angie started feeling woozy. She stumbled to the bed and sat down.

"What's the matter?" George asked.

"I don't know. Maybe I'm just tired, or it could be the wine. I've got to lie down."

George went to his bag and pulled out some papers. "Before you go down for the night, I want you to sign these papers. It's authorization to get the body, just in case it is Aldo. If you do it now, I can go early tomorrow, before you wake, in case your still not feeling well and want to sleep in."

"What papers?" Angie slurred. "I can just about keep my eyes open."

"Here," he said, slipping a pen into her hand. "Sign it right here."

"All right, OK, I need to sleep." She scribbled her name on two lines and almost immediately fell asleep.

One paper was the typed suicide note, printed on her own computer. The other was a will, leaving all her assets to George. He had already arranged to have it notarized by an attorney friend of his who would do anything for a few bucks.

He was now ready to dispose of her.

CHAPTER THIRTY-FIVE

When the lights went out in the hotel room, Aldo figured they were there for the night and decided to go back to his place, rather than spend the night in the rain. When he got back, soaked and tired, he found the boys had returned. The approaching storm had frightened them, and they decided the safest place was with their Mensa. They apologized for leaving and promised they would not do it again. Aldo was too tired to argue, and they all went to sleep,

Just before dawn, Aldo awoke and headed back to Shoal Bay, wondering what the new day would bring. Would he reunite with Angie after being apart for too long? Would she accept him after what he had put her through? What was his friend, George, up to?

As Aldo left the room, Eduardo heard the door shut and wondered where he was going so early on such a stormy day. The storm had subsided a bit but he knew it was the calm before the main body of the storm hit the island. He went to the window and watched Aldo ride away in the direction of Shoal Bay. He awakened Melky. "Come on," he said. "Let's go fishing."

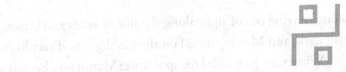

CHAPTER THIRTY-SIX

Martin Alvarez sat on a folded blanket on the beach at Shoal Bay, peering out into the dark waters. It was early morning just before sunrise. The rain had subsided, but it was still quite windy. Suddenly a small light appeared out on the sea, just barely visible and moving slowly along the coast. Martin pulled a small flashlight out of his satchel and began flicking it on and off. The boat with the light turned and headed directly toward shore. It was a small fishing boat, and when it was near shore, two men jumped into the water and pulled it close and secured it with a line. The three men shook hands and embraced, speaking Spanish.

"Is he coming?" Rico said.

"Yeah, mon," Martin answered. "He should be here soon. I told him five."

"Good," replied Rico. "We will wait up there, in the reeds, you keep his attention, we'll take care of him."

"Good," said Martin, as the two others picked up the blanket and walked up the sand, away from the water.

Aldo had arrived at the hotel just in time to see George emerge from his room and head toward the beach. George was wearing shorts, a t-shirt and a Mets baseball cap. Aldo followed him, keeping his distance. When they came down the path toward the shore, George took a sharp right and headed up the beach. Aldo followed along, staying out of sight along the line of reeds and brush. It was still dark, and Martin turned on the flashlight to direct him.

When George reached the spot where Martin was, he stopped. He and Martin shook hands and Martin asked him if he had the money for the gun. While George was reaching in his pocket, the two thugs quickly were behind him. They threw the blanket over his head and, just as quickly, plunged steel blades through the cloth. George moaned and fell to the sand. A large rock crashed down on the blanket where George's head was. The man raised it and struck again. The blanket, now covered with patches of blood, stopped moving. Then, the three men picked up the body and carried it out to the boat.

"Go get the woman!" Aldo heard them say, as he crouched nearby. He was in shock after seeing his friend brutally murdered.

Two of the men headed up the path toward the hotel. Aldo realized who they were going after. He had to do something to stop them from going to the hotel to abduct his wife.

When they had passed by him a good distance, Aldo jumped out of the brush onto the path and yelled to the men. "Murderers! I saw you bastards!." He waved his arms at them. They turned and looked in his direction, trying to see who had called to them.

Startled that someone else was there on the beach at this hour and had seen them, they started to run after him.

Aldo ran back down toward the beach and made a quick turn and headed along the shore with the hoodlums chasing him. Rico, waiting by the boat, had heard the commotion. When he saw the others chasing Aldo, he started after him, too.

It was still dawn and the morning light was just breaking. The men could barely see Aldo as he ran ahead of them.

Aldo figured that he could not outrun them, so he turned sharply and headed into the water. He was hoping his college experience on the swim team and his daily swims would help him now. He felt he was a stronger swimmer than runner.

The men apparently never saw him go into the water and ran right by. Aldo stayed low in the water, bobbing in the waves, and peering onto the beach, until the men were out of sight. He waited a few minutes, treading water, and then slowly came back ashore and headed toward the hotel, hoping he would get there before his pursuers.

Before long, Rico and his buddies realized that whoever they were chasing had eluded them, and headed back to get Angie. They were being paid to take care of both George and his girlfriend and believed they had better finish the job no matter who saw them.

When they got to the hotel, Rico went to the room while the others waited, not wanting to cause suspicion if anyone was awake at that hour. He tried the door. It was locked, so he moved over to the small patio and tried the slider. That was unlocked, so he slid it open and cautiously entered the darkened room clutching the blade he had plunged into George. He listened for any sound, but all was quiet. He felt the wall for a light switch and when he came to one, flicked it on. The room was empty. He slowly moved into the bedroom and turned on the light there also. The bed had been slept in, but now was empty. He heard a noise from the bathroom and clenched the knife tighter, thinking he now had his prey cornered. He cautiously pushed that door open, switched on the light and stepped back. Then he heard a toilet flush in the adjoining suite, and realized that that was where the sound he had heard was coming from. He gave the suite another look around and decided whoever had been there, was gone.

CHAPTER THIRTY-SEVEN

Aldo struggled to support Angie as they moved along the beach. She was still in a daze from the drug George had given her, and did not realize it was her husband of 25 years who had aroused her from her bed and dragged her out into the night, claiming someone was coming to kill her. Even if she was in an alert state, it would have been hard for even her to recognize him with his dreadlocks and native appearance.

Aldo had beaten his adversaries back to the hotel by minutes, and had no time to try to convince her who he was. He had physically dragged her out of the room down to the beach, and now was headed to a spot he hoped would give them refuge. The beach house where he had last been with his wife was just a short distance up the beach, and he hoped it was unoccupied. Even if someone were there, he thought, he could hide somewhere else on the property, or maybe whoever was there could help him.

The sun was coming up as they approached the path that led up to the house. A short way up the path there was a gazebo with a hammock. Aldo lifted Angie and laid her in the hammock. She sunk into it and was barely visible. "Shh," he whispered to her. "Stay here, I'll be right back." Angie nodded and fell back asleep, not comprehending what was happening.

Aldo approached the house cautiously. It was dark inside and there were no vehicles around the front. He thought it looked vacant, but he realized he had better be sure. He picked up a small stone and tossed it at a bedroom window. The glass didn't break, but it made a loud enough noise so that anyone who might be inside could have heard it. He waited in the tall grass. Nothing stirred inside. He threw another stone and when there was no reaction from within, he made his way up the back steps onto the patio. He tried the door. It opened. He remembered the island was still a peaceful, crime free place where hardly anyone locked their doors, except the tourists.

Once inside, he quickly remembered the layout and searched around without putting a light on. He soon knew no one was there and made his way back to retrieve Angie. He picked her up out of the hammock, carried her back to the house and put her in one of the bedrooms. She still didn't recognize him, even though she was starting to come out of the stupor that George had put her in.

Aldo realized he had to do something to reunite with his wife if they were going to escape from whoever was chasing them. He went into the bathroom, and in the dim morning light that was now starting to light the house, he fumbled around for a cutting object. He remembered from when he was last there that there was a basket of personal items under the sink for any guests who needed them. He found it easily. In it there was a razor and scissors. He stared in the mirror and decided he had to lose Mensa Jones and become Aldo Ferrari again. In a matter of minutes, the dreadlocks and beard were gone. He tried to arrange his hair as it had been when he ran off to end it all. As he was finishing, he heard a noise behind him. He turned quickly as the bathroom door opened, and saw Angie staring at him in disbelief. He saw her almost faint and he grabbed onto her and held her close.

"Yes," he whispered to her. "It's me."

"Al, Aldo?" she said as she looked into his eyes. "Why, where have you been? I thought you were dead. I found the note."

"I know," he answered. "I'm so sorry, I missed you so. I love you."

When she had awakened and looked around, Angie thought she had been dreaming and that the past months had never happened. She was still on vacation at the beach house where she and Aldo were staying. It took a few minutes before her head cleared and Aldo convinced her it was real, and that he was alive. He explained how he was rescued and lived in the village. He told her about his job at the library and how he followed her activities over the Internet. "Why were you giving George the money?" he asked.

"I guess he was in trouble financially. There were people hounding him for money. I was just trying to help him out."

"And why did you come back here?" he asked.

"George found that a body had been found in the ocean here, and he said it may be your body. We came here to check it out. I don't know what happened last night. I passed out. How did I get here?"

"I found you at the hotel," He explained. "Some men attacked George on the beach, and they were coming after you. I got there first and brought you here. I figured we would be safe here, at least for a while. Do you know who they are?"

"I don't, but some men chased us out of the house back home and followed us to the airport. I was terrified. Where is George?"

"I'm not sure," he said. "They beat him up and put him in a boat."

"Oh, my God!" she cried. He held her tighter.

After a while they made their way back into the living room area and talked more about the events since they were separated.

"What are we going to do now?" Angie finally asked.

Aldo thought they should stay where they were, until they had an escape route if they were still being chased. From the rear patio, they would be able to see if anyone was approaching from the beach, and the road up to the front of the house was also visible. He felt they could be safe there and could hide easily if anyone approached. He hoped no one knew where they were.

CHAPTER THIRTY-EIGHT

An hour earlier, in the boat anchored just offshore, there was a slight movement under the blood- stained blanket. George slowly regained consciousness and, as he did, felt a sharp stinging pain under his right armpit. He winced. Miraculously, the knives had missed any vital organs and only gave him some nasty gashes. His head ached from the blows he had taken. But, he was alive. He slowly slid the heavy blanket off himself and took a deep breath. Another stabbing pain made him reach for his side. He gathered himself, looked around, and realized he was alone in a small boat near the shore. He looked over the side and thought he was in only a few feet of water. He raised himself up and slid over the side into the water. The sea brought him back to reality. He stood up and trudged ashore, falling on the sand when he was clear of the water. He wondered what had happened and if he could make it back to the hotel.

George was only on the shore a few minutes when he heard voices coming up the beach. He realized he should hide and dragged himself into the tall reeds away from the beach and lay low. He was in serious pain and it took every effort for him to remain still and silent.

When Rico and his pals realized George was gone, they started cursing in Spanish and running up and down the beach looking for him, not thinking he was only a dozen yards away. It was still too dark to see the tracks George had made in the sand as he went for cover. George had kept himself well hidden and after a while, the men got into the boat and sailed off.

After lying low for some time, George finally struggled to his feet and, although still in pain, tried to make his way back to the hotel to get help. He miscalculated and started in the wrong direction, away from the path to the hotel and in the direction of the beach house where Aldo and Angie were hiding out. He had not gotten far when he fell again from pain and exhaustion.

CHAPTER THIRTY-NINE

It was almost 9:00 a.m. Aldo and Angie were still talking about the events of the past months. They were in the back den of the house, from where they had a view of the beach and the ocean. Aldo kept checking for activity in the area. It was raining again and the wind was picking up as the storm moved closer to the island. Out on the water he could see a small boat. In it were what looked like a few fishermen. He grabbed a pair of binoculars off the mantle and went out onto the patio. Outside, he scanned the horizon and soon had the boat in his viewfinder. As he focused, he was surprised to see that the men on the boat were Rico and company. They also had binoculars and were looking at an object on the shore with serious interest. Soon, they seemed to get very animated, waving and pointing toward the object and then turned the boat toward shore and started heading in.

Aldo turned his binoculars to see what they were so interested in. He couldn't get a good view, so he moved around the patio to the other side of the house. From there he had a direct view up the beach. When he focused in on the object on the beach, his heart stopped. It was George. He was kneeling with his legs under him trying to get up.

Instinctively, Aldo ran down the stairs and down the path to the beach in a desperate attempt to try to reach his friend before the killers did. He ran along the dunes, trying to keep out of the sight of the men. The boat was moving slowly in the heavy seas created by the approaching storm, so Aldo figured he could get to George first, but had no idea what he would do then.

Just as Aldo neared George, the men in the boat spotted him. They were still 50 or so yards off shore, but one of the men started firing a pistol at them. Bullets were hitting the sand as Aldo reached George, grabbed him and started pulling him to cover over the dunes just beyond them. Two of the men jumped out of the boat and waded toward shore. The third stayed with the boat and kept firing. Bullets whizzed past them as Aldo pushed George over the top of a small sand dune and dove over himself, the dune shielding them from the gunfire. The men kept coming. From here, there was nowhere else to run. George was spent, unable to move, and Aldo was not going to leave him there to be murdered. The only thing left for him now was to stand and fight. He looked around for something to fight with, but saw nothing but sand. He held his breath, waiting for the men to come over the hill, waiting for the battle he knew he could not win. Two or three minutes passed. Aldo waited. Another two minutes passed that seemed like forever. Then he heard a voice from the beach that sounded amplified.

"Put down your weapon!"

Aldo stood slowly and looked over the top of the dune. There was another boat beside the thug's boat. It was much larger and had flashing lights and large writing across the bow. Aldo could make out the words, "Coast Guard". He thought they most likely were attracted by the gunfire and were investigating. The two men that were on the beach had disappeared, or at least Aldo couldn't see them. He wanted to rush out of his hiding place but thought it would be hard for him to identify himself and he would face interrogation if he did so. He thought about Angie back at the beach house. He was perplexed as to what he should do, and before he could decide, the patrol boat started pulling away with the other boat in tow.

Aldo looked over at George lying face down in the sand. He crawled over to him, and tried to turn him over on his back. As he did, he saw blood trickling from a small hole behind his ear. When he rolled him on his back, he saw George's eyes were wide open, staring at the sky. He put his hand on George's throat to feel for a pulse. There was none. A bullet had apparently found its mark. After being stabbed, beaten and shot, George had finally succumbed.

Aldo held his old friend for a long moment. What, he wondered, had George done to deserve this? How was Angie involved? He thought about covering the body until he could return for it. Then, he thought about his wife, alone at the beach house. He left the body on the dunes and headed back.

CHAPTER FORTY

As Aldo slowly made his way along the beach, back to the house where Angie was waiting , the horror of seeing his life long friend brutally murdered overtook him. He fell to his knees, wretched and vomited in the sand. When he recovered he stood and continued on, wondering how he would tell Angie, and how she would take it. The wind and rain whipped in his face as he walked up the stairs and across the patio to the rear door. He paused a moment to gain his composure, and then he opened the door. He walked inside and saw Angie sitting on the sofa, a very frightened look on her face. He turned to look behind the door, where she was staring, and faced a large handgun, pointed at his head.

"Well, my friend," said Rico. "We finally meet. Just who are you?"

Before Aldo could speak, the other man emerged from the side room. He grabbed him from behind and pushed him to the floor. He took off his belt and bound Aldo's hands behind him. Rico bent over him and asked, "Now, where is your friend?"

"George?" Aldo replied, his face pushed against the floor. "He's dead. You killed him." Angie let out a loud sob.

"Where, where eess the body?" the other man asked in broken English.

"Back behind the dunes, where you were shooting at us," Aldo said. "I'll show you, if you let her alone."

Rico thought a moment, and then said to the other man, "No, Lugo, you go check it out. I'll stay with these two."

Lugo bounded out the door and down the patio stairs toward the beach. The storm was now Intensifying, and a heavy rain was blowing across the island.

Aldo lay motionless on the floor with Rico's gun pointed at him. Angie lay on the couch under Rico's leering watch. They wondered what would happen next.

Aldo finally spoke. "Why did you have to kill him. What did he do to you?" he said in a soft voice, not wanting to irritate his captor, but seeking answers in this mysterious drama.

Rico paused for a while, wondering if he should answer. "This man, Macklin, is he your friend? He killed someone, back in the States. He tried to run away, I think he was also going to kill this woman, too," Rico said, nodding toward Angie. "He tried to poison her last night. My friend Martin told me someone at the café saw him put something in her wine when she was not at the table. He is a bad man. How do you know him? Why would you try to save him? Risk your own life. This is foolish."

Aldo thought about the money missing from Angie's bank account and why they had come here now. Rico's story started to make some sense. "But, why do you need to hold us now. She is my wife. She had nothing to do with any killings. I was just trying to help my friend. I had no idea he was involved with murders. And he's dead now, so why not let us go?" Aldo pleaded.

"It's not that simple," Rico replied. "I was told to get rid of them both, and now, you know who we are, so you too are a danger. I am only repaying a debt I owe by doing this. It is nothing personal against you people. Please understand this."

"Please, we will pay you more. We have money. Let us go," Aldo tried again.

"No," said Rico. "I wish it were that easy, but it's not money. It's a family matter."

Aldo had no answer for this, and lay helpless on the floor.

Lugo made his way through the downpour, back into the house. He wiped the rain from his face with his shirt and said, "It's true, the man is dead. I buried him in the dunes."

Angie gasped.

"So, that part is done. What do we do with these two?" Rico asked.

The men started speaking in both Spanish and broken English, but Aldo made out a few words. "Pier, rocks, over the edge into the water." It did not sound good. He tried to roll over and get up, but Rico pushed him down again, jabbing the pistol in his back.

"Don't be stupid! I will shoot you both right here!" Rico snarled.

The men stopped talking, after seeming to agree on a plan. Lugo pulled Aldo up on his feet, and Rico grabbed Angie by the arm and pulled her off the couch. They pushed them through the doorway and out onto the patio. The wind was howling now and a heavy, tropical rain was blowing hard across the island. They went down the steps and toward the water. When they got to the beach, they turned right and proceeded up the shoreline, the two thugs pushing Angie and Aldo along through the storm. After a short distance, they came to the path that lead up to the pier, the place where the land fell off into the sea. It was the spot where Aldo attempted to end his life months earlier.

"NO TRESPASSING -- AREA CLOSED" read the sign on the fence blocking the path to the platform.

Aldo's heart skipped a beat as he remembered the last time he passed this point. Lugo shoved him and Angie past the barrier and out onto the platform. Rico followed. The deck of the platform was only 12 feet wide and 16 feet long. Almost all of the railings were gone, long since rotted or blown away by storms. The strong winds were rocking the pier back and forth, and it was difficult to keep one's balance. The sea raged against the rocks below.

Rico pointed the gun at Aldo and motioned for him to back up toward the edge. Once again, desperate, Aldo knew he had no choice but to fight. The wind rocked the platform again, and Aldo lunged toward Rico. The gun fired as the two fell to the floor of the platform. Lugo regained his balance and moved to try to help Rico. As he did, he felt an object hit his throat. He staggered back, as he felt warm blood oozing from a hole in his neck. Twenty yards away, just off the pier, Eduardo drew another deep breath and blew another dart from his blowgun. This one hit Rico between the eyes. Dazed, he dropped the gun and tried to stand. There was a loud crack as rotted timber on the pilings below snapped under the weight of the struggle above and the blast of the hurricane force winds. The platform tilted at a 45-degree angle. Aldo felt himself slipping toward the edge and grabbed onto Rico. Angie grabbed them both as she slid by. Lugo, who was closest to the edge, clawed at the rotted floor, but had no chance and fell off into the sea. Eduardo and Melky, who had been searching for Aldo since he left them before dawn, emerged from the brush and raced onto the platform to help their friend. As they stepped on the rain-soaked timbers, Melky slipped and slid. Somehow, Eduardo stopped himself and grabbed on to his brother by his shirtsleeve. They were now all fighting for their lives, all on the edge.

Eduardo, the strongest of them all, slowly inched his way backward, struggling to hold on to Melky. The rain and wind now made it almost impossible to see the others, even though they were only a few feet away. He finally got a foot off the platform and onto solid ground. With a hard jerk, he yanked his little brother up the ramp and rolled him off the shaking pier. Rico, with his own blood nearly blinding him, tried to kick Aldo lose from his grip on his leg. Aldo started to slip away but caught his arm around one of the remaining posts of the dilapidated platform. Angie desperately clung to him. Rico, his face covered with blood, tried to stand. But as he did, the gale force wind toppled him sideways and he fell over the side. His scream faded into the howling wind as he fell onto the rocks below.

Eduardo now tried to reach his friend clinging to a post four feet away. He could not stand because of the wind, so he lay down and stretched his legs out onto the platform as far as he could. Melky did his best to hold on to his brother's arm as he too lay in the mud. Aldo could just reach the outstretched leg and grabbed it. He yelled to Angie, "Go!" and she reached past him, grabbed Eduardo's leg and, crawling, inched up the planks until Melky could hoist her onto solid ground. She immediately turned and grabbed onto the boys for more security as Aldo tried to follow her to safety. The platform rocked severely in the wind. Another loud crack was heard from below and the pier started falling into the sea. Aldo started slipping backward. Eduardo reached out and caught his arm as the structure fell away. Dangling over the edge, Aldo strangely remembered his last fall from this spot. He knew he would never survive again. He looked up and saw Angie reaching for him. She was leaning precariously, trying to reach him. She lunged forward to grab for him and as she did, she slipped. Eduardo reached out to catch her, but he missed and she tumbled past Aldo. Her husband reached for her arm as she slid by. He could not grab onto her and she fell over the edge and into the raging sea below.

Aldo shouted, "No!!" as Eduardo grabbed his arm and pulled him to safety. He wanted to let go and follow her as grief overcame him.

Aldo wept uncontrollably as the three huddled together in the storm, wondering what had happened. What had brought them there.

Aldo and the two boys soon got themselves together and made their way down the cliffs, trying to see if there was any sign of life in the pounding surf. After a frantic search, they finally gave up and made their way back to town and the security of Aldo's room.

The boys explained how, after searching for Aldo, they remembered that he had told them that he was at Shoal Bay the day before. They had arrived there and, as they were searching for Aldo, spotted Lugo on the beach and followed him to the beach house. They waited until they all left the house and then followed them to the pier.

They talked for a while and then, exhausted, the boys fell asleep. Aldo could not. He felt terrible guilt for ever leaving his wife alone, and eventually, he felt, causing her death. Who were these men who were chasing them? Who had sent them here? Who was it that George had killed and why? Was it all connected to his own insurance scam plan?

He vowed to find out. He had to find out who had brought them to the edge.

CHAPTER FORTY-ONE

The platform rocked back and forth, the wind howling and the rain blinding them. Aldo watched the two thugs fall to their deaths. Angie was leaning over the edge to try to pull him back to safety. The platform shook again and she started falling. Aldo grabbed her arm as she slid by him, Eduardo grabbed them both and started pulling them up. Slowly, they inched back to safety as the platform fell away into the sea. They held each other tightly as they huddled together in the storm, all safe together at last. Then Aldo snapped awake and quickly realized he had been dreaming. Angie was not there. She was gone! She had fallen to her death hours before. The short time he had spent with her flashed through his mind.

"Why, Why?" Aldo thought. "What had George done to put his and her lives in jeopardy?" He had to find out. He knew he could not be at peace until he discovered what had happened.

Where would he start? He remembered Rico's words about settling a family debt, but what did that have to do with George and Angie? He thought to go back to the hotel room and see what Angie and George had left behind. Perhaps there were some clues to the mystery there.

By sunrise the next day, the storm had subsided and the island was calm again. Aldo rose early and headed for the Allamar Beach Club. Many islanders were already out, checking and repairing damage the storm had done. When he arrived at the hotel, he stayed undercover as he maneuvered his way around the outside of the unit where George and Angie had stayed. He went to the small window in the rear that he had escaped through. It was still open. He climbed in and started looking around.

There, in one of the bedrooms was Angie's purse, lying on the floor. He picked it up and opened it. There was about $300 and her credit cards. Aldo knew he could use these in his attempt to find her pursuers. He went to the other room and started checking George's things when he came across two pieces of paper that looked like legal documents. One was the suicide note, signed by Angie. Aldo wondered about this.

"She never told me about this when we were together at the beach house," he thought. "But she said she remembered nothing about that night." The other paper looked like a will, with George as beneficiary.

Aldo remembered again what Rico had said about George. It all started to make more sense. Going quickly through George's things, he found his wallet and stuffed it into his own pants pocket. On the nightstand he spotted the bottle of doping agent. He wondered what it could be and then remembered Rico's story about George putting something in Angie's drink. He put it in his pocket to check out later.

Aldo was about to search further when he heard someone approach the door. He could see two people outside. One was fumbling with a key ring. He quickly grabbed the papers, as well as Angie's purse and went back into the bathroom, and climbed out of the window he had come in.

CHAPTER FORTY-TWO

Back in his room, Aldo kept going over in his mind the events on the morning when his wife and friend had died. There were three men, he remembered. Rico and Lugo had fallen to their deaths from the pier. The other, he recalled, had been on the boat that was towed away by the Coast Guard. Aldo thought he looked familiar and then recalled that he looked like the cab driver that picked up George and Angie at the airport. Was he still in custody? He would certainly have information about what had happened.

The boys were now awake and Aldo had a long talk with them to try to ease their fears.

"Who were those men?" Eduardo asked.

"I'm not sure. But I'm going to find out."

"And the woman, who was she?"

"That was Angie, my wife. I told you about her. She was a wonderful woman." Aldo tried to control his emotions and fought back tears.

"We're sorry," Eduardo said. "We tried to save her."

They all huddled together in a comforting embrace until Aldo said, "You guys have to get back to the village. It will be safe for you there. I am going to get to the bottom of this and don't want you in danger."

"We can help," said Melky.

"We will!" Eduardo stated.

"No, listen to me. You have to return to your home. That's it. Now get your things together," Aldo said sternly. The two boys reluctantly agreed.

Aldo accompanied the boys back to their village and spent a few days there grieving for his wife and friend. He spent hours alone, recalling what had happened, or with Harry Potts, the elder who had helped him. He wondered what his next move would be, and then decided to look for Mr. Martin Alvarez. He left the village with a supply of his "medicine" and headed back to The Valley, determined to find answers.

CHAPTER FORTY-THREE

Aldo's first stop, he thought, should be the police station. Perhaps Angie's body had been recovered. Maybe they knew Rico or the others. It was the logical place to start.

At the police station, a plain, two-story building across from the library, he spoke with the clerk, Sgt. Luther Barnes. "Can I help you?" the sergeant asked.

"I hope so," Aldo said. "Last week, on Thursday, I was down near Shoal Bay on the beach when I heard what sounded like gunfire. When I went to check it out, I saw a man in a boat being taken away by what looked to be the Coast Guard. I am trying to find out who that man was. I thought you might have some record of the situation."

"Well, if it was the Coast Guard patrol, you would have to check with them," the officer said, as he looked through a log in front of him. "I see no record of an arrest for that day. Wasn't that the day of the storm?"

"Ah, yes it was," Aldo said. "I also heard that a woman fell into the sea during the storm. Has her body been recovered?"

"I also have no record of that. Where did you hear this?" Barnes asked.

"Oh, at the store this morning. It could have been just a rumor," Aldo said, not wanting to raise further suspicions. "Where is the Coast Guard patrol located?"

"Their office is right down those stairs," Barnes said, pointing to a staircase on the left.

"Thanks," Aldo said and proceeded down to the lower level. There he encountered another man in uniform who looked weather-beaten like an old sailor, and he inquired again about the gunfire.

The man looked at Aldo warily and asked, "Who are you, and why would you be interested in this?"

Aldo thought fast and said, "I'm George Macklin. I was staying at the Allamar Beach Club. I was out for a walk on the beach. I wondered why someone was shooting and hoped no one got hurt. Your patrol boat took him away. Do you know who he was?"

The officer stared at him again. "I don't think this should be a concern of yours, Mr. George Macklin," he said and started to walk away.

Aldo grabbed his arm. "It is a concern of mine," he said sternly, looking the man in the eyes. The officer turned and stared back at Aldo. "And why would that be, sir?"

"He was shooting at me!"

"Again, I ask you, why?"

"That's what I'm trying to find out!" Aldo explained.

"Well, you're not going to find that out here," the officer said.

"You took him away. You must have some record of who he was."

"He said his boat was in trouble, and he was firing his gun to attract attention. We towed him to dock. No reason to arrest him," the officer stated.

"What dock? Where?" Aldo asked.

"Down at Sandy Ground, he tied up there," the old man replied.

"And you don't know who he is?"

The man looked at Aldo curiously and said, "No, no, mon, I don't."

"Thanks," Aldo said and walked back up the stairs and out of the building.

He then went across the street to the library. Because of his new appearance, the receptionist looked at him curiously. When she finally recognized him, she said sarcastically, "Ah, Mr. Jones, it is nice to see ya. Did ya forget ya had a job?"

"No. With the storm and all, I thought we would be closed a while," Aldo replied, walking right past her to the back room where the computer was.

"That was four days ago," she shouted to him. "That bathroom is getting very stinkin'!"

Aldo ignored her and sat down at the PC. He logged onto the Internet and went to a search engine. He took the bottle out of his pocket and typed in the name on the label: Gamma Hydroxyl Butyrate. "It is also used illegally either as an intoxicant or as a date rape drug," read the line in the third paragraph.

Rico was right, Aldo thought. But why would his best friend want to do this to his wife? Then he thought of the papers he found that were signed by Angie. Was this why he wanted her subdued?

Aldo walked out of the library, right past the front desk, without saying a word.

"Mr. Jones," shouted the receptionist. "What about the bathroom??"

CHAPTER FORTY-FOUR

artin Alvarez sat at the bar at Johnno's, a local tavern at Sandy Ground. He had been keeping a low profile since the day he last saw Rico. He wondered what had happened after he had been towed in by the Coast Guard Patrol, and why Rico had not been in touch with him. Did Rico and his partner finish the job? Did he go back to San Juan without settling up with him? These were questions he had no answers for, until the patrol officer strolled in the bar and sat down next to him.

"Martin, my friend," started Sergeant Graves. "I've got some news for you. Your friend Rico won't be getting in touch with you. His body was found this morning over on the beach at Meads Bay. You wouldn't know what happened to him, would you?"

Martin appeared calm, but was shaking inside. "How would I know?" he said, slowly taking a long gulp of his beer.

"Also," continued Graves, "there was a gentleman in my office this morning looking for you, a Mr. George Macklin. You know of him?"

"George Macklin?" thought Martin. "Didn't they kill him? Or did he kill them?" Again he wondered what had happened.

"Do you know him?" Graves asked again. "He seemed very interested in finding you."

"No, how would I know him, mon?" Martin shot back. "Who is he?"

"He looked like a tourist, perhaps from the States. Said he was shot at by someone in the vicinity of where we found you, on the day of the storm."

"Did he think I was shooting at him?"

"Were you?" Graves said, looking into Martin's eyes.

"No, no, I told you why I was shooting."

"Well, my friend, you should be careful. We don't want trouble here on the island, ya know." He put his big hand on Martin's shoulder. "If you need any help, I want you to call me," Graves said as he slid off the barstool and then walked out the door.

Martin ordered another beer and a shot of tequila, and considered what he should do about George Macklin.

CHAPTER FORTY-FIVE

After leaving the library, Aldo rode his scooter to Sandy Ground, an inlet where many fishermen on the island came into the docks to sell their catches, repair or restock their crafts or spend some downtime chatting with their fellow fishermen.

Aldo walked up and down the docks, checking out each boat, each fisherman, looking for something familiar, not realizing the man he was looking for was only a short walk away at Johnno's. All the boats looked the same to him. When he asked some fishermen about a boat that was towed in four days before, no one would offer any information.

Then Aldo remembered the first time he saw Martin, the cabby, picking up George and Angie from the airport. He decided to try his luck there.

He rode his scooter to the airport, a short distance away. He sat around for a few hours looking for signs of Martin, but he never showed. He spoke to some other cabbies, and some knew of Martin, but said they had not seen him for days. They suggested he might be at Blowing Point, the port where the ferries from St. Maarten docked and departed from. Since it was well past sundown, Aldo decided to wait until the next day to check it out.

Again Aldo spent a restless night. Thoughts of Angie, George, Martin, Rico and the pier kept him awake.

CHAPTER FORTY-SIX

Blowing Point is on the opposite side of the island from Shoal Bay. You can see St. Maarten from the docks, and it is a short ferry ride to the larger island. Many tourists fly in to the St. Maarten airport and take the ferry over to Anguilla. There is a lot of activity there when the ferry is scheduled to arrive or depart, as cabbies vie for fares and relatives pick up or drop off family. The few rental car companies on the island have representatives there to offer their services, and some hotels and resorts have shuttles awaiting their guests.

Near the docks the main terminal building houses the country's customs checkpoint and welcoming center. A short distance away is a group of storage warehouses.

Aldo parked his scooter at the far end of the small parking lot and walked down to the dock area, where a half-dozen men were standing around chatting, perhaps waiting for the ferry to arrive. They were all natives, most in dreadlocks and some in jeans and t-shirts.

When Aldo approached, one of them seemed to notice him coming, and immediately left the group and hurried toward the pier. Aldo recognized him as one of the men who had chased him on the beach a week earlier. It was Martin Alvarez.

"Hey!" Aldo called, but Alvarez never turned around. Instead, he picked up his pace. He went down the walkway toward the pier where the boats docked, turned abruptly and darted toward the warehouses. Aldo ran after him, but when he rounded the corner of one of the buildings, Martin was gone. Aldo thought he had to go into one of these doors as he looked down the row of six entrances to the various warehouses. The first one he tried was locked, so he thought Martin could not be in here, unless he locked it behind him. Two doors down, the door was wide open and Aldo cautiously looked in. It was dark inside, except for a shaft of sunlight coming from a window in an upstairs loft. He stepped inside and waited a minute until his eyes adjusted to the darkness. The room was a large open area with boxes and crates strewn everywhere. There was a pulley and rope hanging from a beam, apparently to hoist items up to the loft area. Aldo stood motionless for a few minutes, as he looked around. Although he saw no one, he had an eerie feeling that someone was in there with him.

Suddenly, something moved in a far corner. Aldo made out the outline of a person moving across an open space toward the far wall. He started in that direction. As he moved across the dirt floor, he stumbled and fell over some boxes. Before he could get up, a man was over him pointing a long knife in his face. "Are you looking for me, mon?" Martin asked menacingly.

Aldo stared up at the blade in his face and then into Martin's eyes. "Yes, yes I was," he stammered.

"Why!" Martin retorted. "How do I know you?"

Aldo thought his best bet was to tell the truth. Maybe Martin needed answers, too, about his friends.

"I was on the beach at Shoal Bay last week when you were after that man, the American."

"That was you? No, that man looked like a Rasta."

"Yes, I shaved, cut my hair. Why were you chasing him?"

Martin looked at Aldo closer. Maybe, there was a resemblance, he thought. "Well, if you were there," he said, "maybe you know what happened to my friends, Rico and Lugo, I haven't seen them since."

"I do," Aldo said. "Let me up, we can talk."

Martin seemed suspicious, but since he had the weapon, he had the upper hand. He moved off Aldo cautiously. "Don't do anything stupid, mon," Martin said sternly. "I will use this!" He flashed the blade in Aldo's face.

"No, don't worry," Aldo said. "I have no problems with you. I'm just looking for some answers. My wife and friend are dead. I want to know why. That's all."

"That woman is your wife?" Martin asked. "Why was she with him, the one we were after?"

"He was a friend of mine. They came here from the States, I suppose looking for me. It's a long story. But why were you and Rico after him?" asked Aldo again.

"I don't know. My friend, Rico, called me to help him with some business, bad business, I guess. I didn't know a woman was involved, or you. And, what happened to them?"

"They found us after my friend was shot. He died out on the dunes," Aldo started slowly. "They decided to throw us off the high platform near Shoal Bay. The storm was just getting bad. The pier started falling. Rico, the other man and my wife fell off. It was terrible." Aldo's voice started cracking as he once again recalled the deaths.

Martin looked at him intently and slowly lowered the knife. There was a long silence.

"I would just like to find out why, why Rico wanted to kill George, and then us," Aldo finally said.

"He never told me what his reasons were," Martin explained. "He said he needed some help. He has done me favors. I was just helping him."

Aldo backed away and sat down on some boxes. "What do you know about Rico? Where is he from? Here, on the island?" he asked.

"No, mon," Martin replied, now feeling anxious to help Aldo. "He lives in San Juan. I'm not sure exactly where. I know he spent some time in the U.S. I think New Jersey, I'm not sure."

Martin thought a minute, and then continued. "He does have a sister who lives here on the island. She works at Banky's, bartends, I think."

"Where is that?" Aldo asked. "What's her name?"

"Banky's, The Dunes over at Rendezvous Bay. It's a club. Her name is Joanie."

"Could you help me find her?" Aldo asked.

"Look, mon. I told you enough. I could have keeled you. I think I had enough of this. I'm sorry about your wife and friend, so I'm letting you go. Don't cause any more trouble around here. Just go home, Si?"

Aldo shrugged. "Yeah, thanks, I guess," he said. "I appreciate your help and your mercy. I won't bother you again." He held out his hand. Martin reluctantly held out his. The two men shook. Martin vanished out a side door.

Aldo now had a new lead.

CHAPTER FORTY-SEVEN

At Tata's in Lodi, New Jersey, there was concern among some of the regulars that they had not heard from Mr. Rico Fuentes. Rico was their contact in Puerto Rico and someone they relied on for any business they had there and throughout the Caribbean. He checked on drug shipments, laundered money and was usually dependable for most dirty work, including murder. He would usually report back after completing his assignment, hence the concern that he had not been heard from in over a week. Phone calls to his San Juan apartment went unanswered, and his relatives had not seen or heard from him, either. Mikey decided he should check with his friend in Anguilla.

Sergeant Graves picked up the phone in his office.

"Mr. Graves, this is your pal, Mike calling from New Jersey. How are you?" After exchanging pleasantries, Mikey got to the subject at hand. "Have you seen our friend, Rico? He had some business there on the island, and I was thinking he might have checked in with you."

"Well, my friend," said the sergeant, "I don't think he will be checking in with anyone. Ya see, they found his body a couple days ago."

"No kidding," replied Mikey, a bit shocked. "Do you know what happened to him?"

"Not sure. They pulled his body out of the ocean. But there was a fellow in here soon after, an American, asking some questions. A Mr. George Macklin."

There was a long silence. "What do you know about this Macklin fellow?" Mikey finally asked.

"Not much," said Graves. "Never saw him before. Said he was staying at The Allamar. Thought someone may have been shooting at him. Didn't know why. Was Rico involved with him?"

"Could have been," said Mikey. "Listen. Maybe you could check on Mr. Macklin for me. See if he's still around, there on the island. If you find out anything, give us a call. OK? You know I'll return the favor."

"Sure, sure mon, I'll do that, and let ya know," answered the sergeant.

Mikey was not happy with this news. Now, he figured, George Macklin had killed two of his employees, and was getting to be a real pain in the ass.

CHAPTER FORTY-EIGHT

Aldo rode his scooter down the long dirt road that led to The Dunes. The club was located in a large barn-like building on the beach at Rendezvous Bay. It was operated by Banky Banks, a reggae star who was-well known throughout the Caribbean. He performed there nightly and, on occasions, held concerts in the outdoor arena on the grounds. The Dunes was a popular spot for tourists as well as locals. The club didn't open until 9: 00 p.m. and stayed open for as long as there were people there, usually into early morning.

Aldo parked his scooter and walked up the stairs to the front entrance. He paid the cover charge and went inside. It was dimly lit, and there were a number of small rooms scattered off narrow hallways. In one of the larger rooms was a small stage and some tables for patrons to sit at. Some of the tables were occupied with people sipping cocktails and talking. There were drums and a few guitars on the stage, but no one was performing yet. There was a bar in one of the rooms and there was a male bartender, but no Joanie, the girl Aldo had come to find.

Aldo went in to the bar and ordered a rum and coke, his first drink in over a year, and inquired of the bartender about her. He was told she was indeed working tonight in the lounge on the upper level. He found the stairs up and went up to second level. There were several rooms on that level also, as well as an area that opened out onto a patio. He found the barroom and looked in.

Joanie Fuentes was a very attractive Spanish woman, tall with long dark hair and beautiful hazel eyes. She was probably in her late 30s, Aldo thought, and obviously took care of herself. He left the drink he was drinking on a table, and approached the small bar. There were two others sitting there chatting. Aldo sat down at the bar, away from the others, and when the woman came over, he ordered another rum. She brought him his drink and he sat there for a while, anxiously waiting for a chance to speak to her alone.

After a while, music started coming from downstairs, as Banky started his performance, and the other couple got up and left.

Aldo motioned that he needed another, and when Joanie came over he said, "I'm sorry about your recent loss, Joanie."

She looked at him skeptically. "Do I know you?" she said in a soft voice.

"No, I don't think so, "Aldo replied. "But I met your brother."

"A lot of people met my brother," she said slowly. Then she added, "Some wish they hadn't."

"I was with him when he died," Aldo said.

She looked up quickly from the glasses she was washing in the sink and asked, "What do you mean? He drowned?"

"Yes, I know, but I know what happened," Aldo replied.

A young man came in the barroom and went behind the bar to refill the ice bins. He poured himself a soda and looked like he was going to hang out there for a while.

Aldo asked Joanie, "Can we talk alone somewhere?"

She looked at Aldo intently and said to the young man, "Watch the bar, I'm going out for a smoke." She motioned for Aldo to follow. They went down a back staircase and out onto the beach. It was a typical Caribbean night. There were thousands of bright stars in the sky. They could see the lights of St. Maarten in the distance, across the water. They walked a short way down the beach and stopped.

It was very quiet, except for waves lapping at the shore.

Joanie lit a cigarette and spoke first. "So, who are you and why did you come here?"

"My name is Aldo Ferrari," he started. "Your brother was trying to kill me and my wife, push us off a pier into the ocean, when he fell himself. He took my wife with him. I came here to try to find out why, who he was, why he was after us."

She took a drag on her cigarette, and blew it out. She shook her head slowly. "I'm sorry. My brother was not a good person. I know," she said. "When he came back from the States, he seemed changed. I hardly saw him anymore. He got involved with some bad people. I don't know what they were into. I didn't want to know. Why he was after you, I have no idea. Did you owe them money?"

"No, but my friend, he was killed, too, he may have been involved somehow. That's what I'm trying to find out. Do you know anything about Rico's associates in the States? Where are they from?"

Joanie took another long drag on her smoke.

"I only know Rico lived in New Jersey when he was there," she answered. "Exactly where, I don't know."

"Could you find out?" Aldo asked, "Did he leave anything that might be a clue?"

She paused for a minute, running her fingers through her long dark hair. She thought a minute and answered, "I'm not sure. He has an apartment in San Juan. I am going there Friday to help Mama with the arrangements. She is coming in from the States. I will ask her if she knows anything." She paused again and looked into Aldo's eyes, not knowing if she should trust him. "If you can meet me there," she continued, "maybe there are some answers."

"If you don't mind," Aldo said. "I promise I won't cause any trouble for you or your mama. I just need some answers."

Joanie took a last drag on her cigarette and tossed it in the sand. "Come back to the bar," she said slowly. "I will give you my number and the address. I should be there by noon Friday. Just try not to upset my mother anymore."

"I won't. I promise," Aldo said. "Thank you." They walked slowly back along the sand together, each now with someone to share their grief. As they entered the bar, Banky was singing "Busted in Barbados," and there was a strong smell of marijuana in the air.

CHAPTER FORTY-NINE

The next morning, Aldo went to the airport and booked his flight. Since he had no identification of his own, he used George's name and credit card. He still wanted to stay undercover until he had some answers. He thought he could pass through security with George's license for an ID, because they looked a little alike, and at that time, security at smaller airports was a little lax. He booked an early Friday morning flight to JFK, with a four-hour layover in San Juan. He was very anxious about a return to the States, but he knew that was where George's troubles began, and that's where he hoped he could find the reasons his wife and George were killed.

As soon as Aldo's flight left the runway, headed for Puerto Rico, Martin Alvarez, who had been watching him for three days, phoned Sgt. Graves, who immediately called New Jersey. "Mr. Macklin is on his way," he told the "Shark." "He should be at Kennedy about four this afternoon, on American flight 262 out of San Juan."

"Good job, Sarge," was the reply.

Aldo made it through security and he was on his way. It was a flight he should have taken 13 months ago with Angie by his side. He could not help feeling pain in his heart when he thought of this as his flight lifted off. Could he have done something to change what had happened if he was there with Angie and George? And what did happen? Was George involved in a murder as Rico had said? If so, who had hired Rico to seek revenge? He hoped to find some clues in San Juan before continuing his search for answers at home in the United States.

CHAPTER FIFTY

After landing in Puerto Rico, Aldo went immediately to the ground transportation area, and caught a cab. He had four hours before his connecting flight left for New York. He gave the driver the address, not having any idea where he was going. They left the airport and headed towards the city. After a few miles they turned onto Avenuida Jose De Diego and then onto Calle 38th Street. After four blocks they stopped in front of a tenement house, 1121 Calle 38, the address Joanie had given him. It was a rundown building among many of the same.

Aldo paid the fare and got out. There were people on the street, some just hanging out, and some on their way here or there. Some looked at him oddly, an obvious stranger in this neighborhood. He went up the front stairs and checked out the names on the mail bins. There was no Rico Fuentes. The apartment number on the paper Joanie had given him said 3-B. He made his way up the stairs. There was a smell of Spanish food lingering in the air. There was salsa music coming loudly from somewhere on the second floor. He glanced down the hallway as he passed the second floor landing. A young boy was playing in the hall. He saw Aldo and ran inside one of the apartments. A woman looked out and quickly slammed the door. On the next landing Aldo turned down the hall to 3-B. The door was closed and he knocked softly.

"Who?" A woman's voice asked from inside.

"It's Aldo," he said. "Is Joanie here?" Twenty seconds passed and Aldo was about to knock again. The door opened slowly and Joanie peered out.

"You came," she said. "I didn't think you would."

"I had to," Aldo replied.

"Come in." The apartment was messy, clothes strewn here and there, newspapers left around, and remnants of food and drink, mostly beer, were scattered everywhere. It reminded Aldo of some college dorm rooms he had been in, many years before.

Joanie's mama, an old, wrinkled Spanish woman in a black dress came out of the back room. She stared at Aldo, but said nothing. "Mama, this is the man I was telling you about," Joanie said in Spanish. The woman just nodded at Aldo, who reached out his hand to greet her. She mumbled something to Joanie, and went back to the kitchen.

"We didn't find much that would interest you," Joanie said. "No letters or anything like that, unless she took them already. She didn't like the idea of a stranger looking into our affairs."

"I can understand that," said Aldo. "What about phone calls, where's the phone?"

"Back here, next to the bed."

Aldo went over and looked to see if there were any papers or notes around the phone. There was an old phonebook on the lower shelf of the nightstand. He picked it up, looked at both covers and then opened it to the inside cover. There were numbers and names scribbled on it. He recognized one name, Martin A., and perhaps another, SGT G. Both had an Anguillan area code. Aldo perused the other jottings until he came to one with the area code 908. It was a U.S. number, although Aldo wasn't sure where. After looking through the book for more clues, but finding nothing else, he tore off the cover, folded it and put it in his pocket.

Aldo then looked under the bed where he saw an old wooden

crate. With Joanie watching, he nudged it out and pried it open. Under some girly magazines on top, Aldo found a large satchel. He pulled it out and opened it. It was stuffed with cash, $100 bills. Lots of them. Under the satchel was a 9 mm handgun. "Did you miss this?" Aldo asked as he pointed it out to Joanie.

"I never checked there," she said.

Aldo thought a minute, and then handed it to her. "I'm sure he wanted his mama to have this," he said.

Wide eyed, Joanie agreed. They both then spent another hour going through Rico's things, but there seemed to be nothing more that would be of help to Aldo.

He called a cab to take him back to the airport and was about to leave. He thanked Joanie, and said if she came to the States, to look him up. "Syosset, New York," he told her.

"Maybe If I get through this nightmare, I can return the favor."

Joanie handed him the gun. "Please take this with you," she said.

"What am I going to do with it?" he asked. "I'm going on a plane. I can't take it with me."

"Just get it out of here, please. It frightens me. Get rid of it somewhere."

Aldo took the weapon and the ammo clips. He shoved them in his jacket pocket and said, "OK, I'll ditch it somewhere."

Just as he was leaving, Mama appeared again. She came up to him and said, "Gracias." She grabbed his hand and shook it. She then handed him some photos of Rico. Aldo looked through them. There were three that were taken of him and some men in front of a restaurant. Aldo looked closely. The name on the building was Tata's Supper Club, with a phone number just barely readable. "Can I have these?" he asked.

Joanie repeated the request in Spanish. The old woman nodded.

"Gracias," said Aldo. He leaned over and kissed her. Then he also thanked Joanie and left.

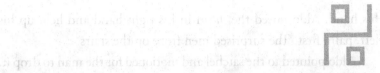

CHAPTER FIFTY-ONE

Aldo went outside on the street to wait for his cab. Just as it pulled up to the curb him, another vehicle, a pickup truck, sped up and double parked in front of the apartments he had just left. Two men got out and went up the front stairs in a hurry. One was young and wearing jeans and a T-shirt. The other was an older man in dress slacks and a jacket. Both were dark-skinned. Aldo watched them from across the street as they went in. He had a strange feeling about them, a bad feeling. He went to the cab and held up one finger to the driver, "Uno momento," he said. The driver nodded his assent.

Aldo made his way slowly back across the street and up the front stairs into the building he had just left. He proceeded cautiously up the first flight of stairs to the second floor landing. The music had stopped and it was quiet. As he rounded the corner and started up to the third floor, he heard shouting and a woman scream. Then there was gunfire. He stepped back down to the landing and took the pistol out of his pocket. He had only fired a gun once in his life. A friend of his, a New York City cop, had once brought him along to a firing range for target practice. That was fun, he thought, this was not. He put the ammo clip in and released the safety.

Suddenly, the two men came around the corner of the third floor landing and started down the stairs, straight at Aldo. The younger man in front was carrying the satchel; the second one had a gun in his hand. Aldo raised the 9mm in his right hand and held up his left, palm first. The surprised men froze on the stairs.

Aldo pointed to the satchel and motioned for the man to drop it. As he did, the second man shielded by the first, decided to challenge Aldo, and started to raise his gun. Aldo took a quick step to his right and squeezed the trigger. The sound and the recoil almost knocked Aldo back down the stairs. The bullet, fired point-blank, struck the man in the chest and he crashed back on the stairs, blood spattering the wall behind him. The gun fell from his grip and rattled down the steps, ending up on the landing below. The other man dropped the satchel quickly. Aldo recovered and motioned for him to move past him down the stairs. With the 9mm pointing at him, the man backed down slowly and, when he reached the landing, picked up the gun and disappeared.

Aldo picked up the bag, stepped over the body and continued up to the third floor. He opened the door to Rico's apartment slowly. He gasped as he saw the two women. Mama was face down on the floor, with a bullet hole behind her left ear. Joanie was spread across the bed, blood oozing from a large, ugly hole under her right eye. Aldo felt for a pulse in each woman. They were both dead.

"Damn, damn!" he yelled, as he bent over Joanie. Then he heard sirens out on the street in the distance. There he was, with a gun in his hand and a satchel of money, and three people dead. It would be tough to explain. He had to get out of there. He figured if he went down the stairs, the man he let go could be waiting. He moved to the kitchen area and saw a door leading out to a fire escape. After undoing multiple locks and latches, he got the door opened, and went out and down the rusted stairs. They stopped four feet from the ground. He threw the satchel to the pavement, jumped off and landed in the alleyway. He got up and retrieved the satchel. He put the gun in his jacket pocket, and thought about getting away as fast as he could.

Police cars were pulling up on the street. Aldo jumped a small fence and went through a maze of alleys, over and around trash cans and dumpsters, until he emerged onto a main thoroughfare, Avenuida De Diego. A city bus was discharging passengers on the opposite corner. He dodged traffic as he crossed the street. He got in line behind the others who were waiting and boarded the bus, not knowing where it was going.

Aldo moved to the rear of the bus and tried to look inconspicuous. He took a seat near a window and picked up a newspaper that was on the seat. He put the paper in front of his face and looked out the window. There, out on the street, he saw something that made his heart stop. Alongside of the bus was the pickup truck that was in front of the apartments. The driver was the man Aldo had let go, and there was another man in the passenger seat. A third man was in the back bed of the pickup. They were all staring at the bus.

Aldo pulled back from the window, and put the paper over his face. "Did someone follow him?" he asked himself. "How could they know he was on that bus?"

The truck moved past the bus, but at the next traffic light it stopped, directly in front of the bus. When the light changed, the pickup didn't move. The bus driver honked the horn. The driver of the truck got out and came around to the door of the bus. The passenger in the truck moved to the driver's seat. The man indicated he wanted to get on, and the driver opened the door. Aldo, peering out from behind the newspaper, cringed.

The man walked slowly toward the rear, checking out each passenger. Aldo dropped the satchel on the floor and moved it under the seat with his foot. He put the paper closer to his face, and leaned against the window pretending to be asleep. His hand reached into his jacket pocket and wrapped around the 9mm, his finger on the trigger. The man passed by slowly, staring at him intently. Aldo tensed. After a few long seconds, the man continued on by and checked the remaining passengers. He then went back up to the front of the bus. At the next stop, the man got off and returned to the pickup that had followed close to the bus. Aldo wondered if he had been recognized, and if they were just waiting for him to get off.

After a few more stops, the bus entered the hotel district. There were tourists and cabs everywhere. Here he would not look out of place, he thought. He looked around and didn't see any signs of the pickup or the men, though he worried they may still be after him, waiting to make their move. Many of the remaining passengers were getting off the bus. He grabbed the satchel off the floor and mingled with the others as he got off and then moved quickly between cars and busses, until he spotted an empty taxi. He got in, and again slumped down in the seat. "The airport," he told the driver.

The cab arrived 30 minutes before his scheduled departure time. He still had a gun and the money to dispose of. He knew he was not allowed to take the gun on board, and the satchel of cash probably would raise the suspicion of a wary scanner and he did not want to risk being detained. He took a wad of bills from the bag and stuck them in his pocket. He then found a bank of lockers on the main concourse, rented one and deposited the satchel and gun there. He thought he could retrieve them at a later time, if he ever came back there.

He boarded his flight for home, thinking about the day's events. Now he was also a killer, being pursued and living on the edge.

CHAPTER FIFTY-TWO

American Airlines flight 262 touched down at JFK at 4:16 p.m., 13 months since Angela Ferrari thought she was bringing her husband home. This time he was onboard and alive, being pursued and also a pursuer. He had no luggage so he went immediately to the car rental kiosk and arranged for transportation, again using George's credit card. He left the airport and headed out onto the Van Wyke Expressway, exiting onto the Long Island Expressway, toward Long Island. He had decided to go back to Syosset to check out the house, not knowing what he would find there, or who might be waiting. He had a strange suspicion that he was being followed. And he was.

When Aldo got to his exit, he thought he should stop and rethink the situation, maybe not go to the house right away, in case someone was tailing him. He hadn't eaten the whole crazy day, so he pulled into a diner right off the highway. He parked, and went inside. He sat at a booth where he could look out the window. The waitress came over and he ordered a sandwich and black coffee.

He checked out everyone coming into the parking lot and into the diner, and to him everyone looked suspicious. When the waitress brought his food, he was so nervous, that he could only nibble at it. He drank the coffee, paid his check and walked out. As he approached his car, he noticed two men standing next to it. Glancing over his shoulder he saw another man right behind him. He sped up past the car and broke into a trot as the men took up pursuit. Aldo ducked between cars, and then ran into a used car lot next to the diner. He dodged this way and that and then hit the ground and rolled under a large SUV. He lay there motionless as legs and feet moved past him. Then, they came back past him again, and then he heard nothing except the traffic in the street.

After fifteen minutes, Aldo decided to venture out of his hiding spot. He raised himself up part way and looked around the lot. When he thought he was safe, he stood up. He felt a sharp blow strike his head before he lost consciousness.

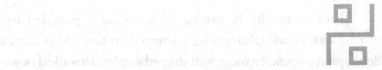

CHAPTER FIFTY-THREE

When Aldo awoke, he was in complete darkness. His head throbbed, and his first thought was that he had lost his sight. He was lying on his side. His legs were unable to move. His hands were bound. There was tape over his mouth. Then he heard the sound of tires on pavement and saw a glimmer of red light on his right. He realized he was in the trunk of a car. They must have been waiting for him when he came out from hiding, he thought. But who were they? Were they connected to the men in Puerto Rico, or to the killers on Anguilla? He worried that he was about to find out.

After an agonizing 40 minutes, the car stopped moving. The engine was shut off. Aldo heard and felt two doors bang shut, and then the trunk opened. Three men looked down at him. One chuckled. They grabbed him, pulled him out and stood him up. His legs were cramped and his knees buckled. When his eyes finally focused, he quickly glanced around and noticed some dumpsters. He saw cars in an adjacent parking lot and thought he might be in the back of a restaurant. The men grabbed him under his arms and dragged him toward the building and down some stairs into a basement. They flicked on some lights. One man grabbed a chair, brought it under a low hanging light and sat Aldo down. A rope was thrown around him and tightened securely. One of the men came up and punched him in the face. Blood trickled from his nose.

"That's for Butch!" he snarled. Aldo winced in pain, but had no idea what he was talking about. After a short time, Aldo heard a door upstairs open. An older, well-dressed gentleman walked slowly down the stairs, spoke to the men in Italian and came over to Aldo. He pulled up another chair directly in front of him. He motioned to one of the men and the tape was yanked off Aldo's face.

Mikey "The Shark" sat down in front of Aldo. "Well, Mr. Macklin, we finally meet," he said slowly.

"Mr. Macklin?" Aldo said. "I'm not George Macklin."

"Sure, sure, you're James Bond."

The other men laughed.

"No, sir, I am not George. He was a friend of mine, until someone killed him," Aldo pleaded.

"Your license says you're George Macklin, you're passport says your George Macklin, you're tickets say your George Macklin, but you're not George Macklin?"

Again a chuckle was heard from the onlookers.

"Look," Aldo started, "I don't know who you are or where we are, but let me try to explain this. George was a friend of mine. Why you were chasing him, I don't know. He and my wife, Angie, came to Anguilla, where I was hiding out."

A puzzled look came to Mikey. "Hiding out?" he said.

"Yeah, it's another story, but I was trying to scam the insurance company, so my wife would get some money, a lot of money. Then she and George came there, to the island, and both got killed. So did the man who killed them, Rico. I was left, and I needed to find out what happened. I took George's credit cards and IDs, used them to buy tickets and get back here. George is dead, really. I was with him when he died on the beach in Anguilla. That's when I met Rico. He tried to kill us, too. He slipped off the pier, along with my wife."

Mikey stared at Aldo and scratched his chin. Then he sat back, thought a moment and said to the other men. "Is Dinuzz upstairs? Go get her."

A few minutes more passed and the door opened upstairs. Aldo saw two shapely legs in high heels coming down the stairs. "Gloria" came over and stood next to Mikey.

"What?" Stephanie asked.

Mikey said, "Is this the guy you fucked in AC, before Butch was knifed."

DiNuzzo looked at Aldo. "Nah, that ain't him," she said.

"Are you sure?" asked Mikey.

"Of course I'm sure. I never seen this guy before."

Mikey motioned her away "All right, see ya," he said abruptly.

Dinuzzo sauntered back up the stairs. Mikey looked puzzled. "So, who are you?" he said.

"My name is Aldo Ferrari," Aldo explained. "As I said, George was my friend. Why were you after him?"

"Your friend owed us some money. Then he killed an associate of mine, slit his throat. That can't happen, without some retribution, you understand. I'm sorry your wife got killed, too, but maybe she was involved, I don't know."

"I don't know either," Aldo replied, "That's what I'm trying to find out."

"OK, the next question," Mikey interrupted. "Where's my money?"

"Your money?" Aldo said.

"Yeah, my 200 grand. See, Rico had two jobs when he left here. One, get Macklin. Two, deposit my cash in my Cayman account. Apparently he never got to the second one. But according to my sources, you got to the dough before they did. Took out one of my guys, too."

Aldo thought before he replied. This could be his bargaining chip, his only one. "I don't have the money," Aldo said slowly. "But I do know where it is."

"Is that right?" Mikey shot back. "Do you want to tell us?"

Aldo remained silent. Mikey asked again, more intently. "My money, where is it?"

Again, Aldo didn't speak.

"Maybe my friends here can convince you that it's in your best interest to cooperate," the "Shark" said menacingly.

"They can try if you want them to," Aldo said. "But I'm telling you, that it may be in your best interest to just let me go get it for you. If you kill me, or fuck me up, that money will rot before you see it."

Mikey leaned back. He motioned to the men again and spoke in Italian. Aldo braced himself for another beating. The men came over to Aldo's chair. One of them reached in his pocket and pulled out a switchblade. He flicked it open to show the long, shiny blade. Aldo figured his ploy had not worked and tensed for the worst. The man bent over and cut the ropes. Aldo, surprised, freed his hands and wiped the blood from his face. Mikey leaned back. He reached into his vest pocket and pulled out two long cigars.

"I like you, Ferrari," he said. "Maybe we can work this out. Smoke?" he asked as he held out a cigar to Aldo.

Aldo waved his hand. "No, no thanks," he said, as he somehow remembered Angie's father many years ago.

"You know," Mikey started, "with Butch and Rico gone, I need someone like you, someone inconspicuous, who can handle a piece, as obviously you can. Someone with some balls, like you, who can do odd jobs, you see. Make some collections, maybe take a trip to the Caribbean once in a while, and just be available when I need you." He paused, lit the cigar and continued, "Besides, we're probably related in some way."

Aldo thought about what the "Shark" was saying. The Caribbean part was especially inviting, since he wanted to go back there occasionally to see the boys, visit the village and replenish his medicine.

"I hate to sound like Marlon Brando," Mikey chuckled. "But this may be an offer you can't refuse."

The late night diners were finishing their cannolis and tiramisus and sipping their sambucas when Aldo walked up the stairs. He gave DiNuzzo a wink as he walked by the bar and out the front door. He looked around and now recognized Tata's from the photo that Joanie's mother had given him. He felt some relief because he had discovered why George and Angie were being chased and ultimately killed. He now knew where the money that he had found in Rico's apartment had come from and why he was being pursued. He had some new friends and a new job. He had gone over the edge.

PART TWO

CHAPTER FIFTY-FOUR

Aldo stood outside Tata's Restaurant thinking it was a beautiful night in New Jersey, if there was such a thing. He was waiting for a ride to bring him back to his car on Long Island. He was thinking about what had just occurred. He had come to an agreement with mobster, Mikey "the Shark" Barbierio, for his freedom, but it came with some stipulations. He could be free to go back to his home in Syosset, but they would be keeping a close watch on him. He knew that they would. Within the next few days, they would arrange for him and another associate to return to Puerto Rico to retrieve the money. Once it was returned and accounted for, they would discuss his compensation and next assignment. They shook hands on these arrangements and, although Aldo was not comfortable with it, it was his way out of a scary situation.

A Lincoln Town Car pulled around front from behind the restaurant and stopped in front of Aldo. Someone inside unlocked the door and rolled down the window, motioning him to get in. Aldo slid into the passenger seat next to the driver, Stephanie Di Nuzzo. "I'll take ya," she said. "The other guys are busy, big poker game. I do all the jobs they don't wanna do."

"Sure," said Aldo, somewhat surprised. "I'm going back to Long Island, over the George Washington Bridge."

"I know," she replied. "They told me how to get there. I think I can remember."

"Good, because I have no idea how I got here," Aldo said.

They made their way down Route 17 and onto I-80, heading toward New York City. After a while Di Nuzzo asked, "I know it ain't my business, but why did they have you tied up like that? You seem like a nice guy."

Aldo thought for a minute and then said, "It's a long story, and it's probably better you don't know."

"Yeah, you're right. But did it have something to do with that Macklin guy?"

Aldo realized she might be able to tell him some more of the details of what had happened to George and Angie, and asked, "You knew him?"

"No, I didn't really know him. I just met him once, at Caesar's, in AC."

Aldo thought for a minute about what was said when he was tied up and how she came down to identify him. "You only met him once, and you had sex with him?"

Now she paused, wondering how to answer. "Well, yeah," she said slowly. "But it was just business, if you know what I mean."

"OK, sure. I guess I do. But they said he killed somebody. Did you know about that?"

She paused again, thinking maybe she should shut up, but then continued, "Yeah, he killed Butch, a friend of mine, a nice guy. He didn't have to do that."

"But why?" Aldo pressed. "Why would he do that? He wasn't a violent man. I knew him all my life."

"Money, I guess. He owed us, I mean he owed my boss, a lot of money. Butch went to collect it, and wound up with his throat slit. Not very nice!"

"So they figured George did it, and went after him, all the way to the Caribbean," Aldo said, mostly to himself.

"Yeah," DiNuzzo replied. "They got connections there. They got connections everywhere. It's hard to hide when you fuck them over."

"I know," Aldo mumbled, recalling his own brief experience with her associates.

Stephanie drove across the George Washington Bridge and continued on the Cross Bronx Expressway, toward the Whitestone Bridge onto Long Island. They talked more about her brief encounter with George, and although she never admitted taking his money, Aldo had a feeling she might have been involved in the whole mess.

The conversation turned to Aldo and his new involvement with the family. "So you gonna be working with us?" Stephanie asked.

"I guess you could call it that."

"Sort of doing Butch's job?" she asked.

"You might say that. I just hope I don't end up like him."

"Yeah, right. You got to be careful in this business. Why do you even want to get involved?"

"Well, at this point, I don't have much choice."

"What do you mean?" Stephanie asked, not really expecting him to tell her.

"Well, again, it's a long story, and let's just say we have a mutual agreement. I have something they want and so they need to keep me on their side."

"Oh, you mean the money?" she said. "Where did you say it was?"

At this point a light went on in Aldo's head. How did she know about the money and his new association if she was just a hooker doing them a favor by giving him a ride. "I didn't, and I won't," he said. "So let's change the subject. Want to stop for coffee?"

"Um, I'd like to, but I really got to get back. They will be waiting for me."

"I bet," Aldo mumbled to himself.

When Stephanie pulled into the diner parking lot, it was after midnight. Aldo was dog tired as he searched his pockets for the keys to the rental car. He couldn't find them and thought he must have lost them somewhere during his struggles, either on the ground or in the trunk. "Pull over here," he motioned to DiNuzzo, pointing to where he left the car. "Wait a minute," he said as he got out. "I might need a ride to my house. It's only a couple blocks from here."

"Sure, whatever," said DiNuzzo.

Aldo looked on the ground where he had hid but couldn't find anything. Then he thought the car they were in might be the same as the one the thugs threw him in and asked her to open the trunk. He checked there and also came up empty. He slammed it closed and got back in the car.

"Can't find em? "she asked.

"No, but my house is five minutes away. Take a right out here," he said as he pointed to the street. As they turned down his street, a strange feeling came over him. He had been away for over a year, done some things he would always regret, and now he was home. Because of his actions, his dear wife Angie was no longer there to console and comfort him. His actions and the ensuing events came back to him, and once again he felt terrible guilt. He thought how alone Angie must have felt when she returned from the island, thinking he was dead. "Damn," he muttered to himself, as he held back his emotions.

"What?" DiNuzzo said. "You OK?"

"Yes," Aldo replied, trying to pull himself together.

"The next house on the left. Pull in the driveway."

When the car came to a stop, Aldo put his hand on Stephanie's shoulder and said, "Thanks a lot. I really appreciate this."

"No problem," she said, looking him in the eyes. "I like you. Anytime you need help, give me a call. I'm usually at the club. And be careful. Those guys don't fool around.

"Sure, thanks again," he replied, getting out of the car.

CHAPTER FIFTY-FIVE

As she drove back to Tatas' in New Jersey, Stephanie's mind kept drifting back to thoughts of Aldo, and that she really meant it when she told him she liked him. It was not in a physical way, but more like a father or brother, neither of which she ever had. She had grown up in Pennsauken, New Jersey, a suburb of Philadelphia, very close to the slums of Camden. Her father had left her mother soon after she was born and never returned. She later discovered he was killed in a mob shootout. Her mother worked all the time to support them, and they lived with her grandparents, who were Italian immigrants. They were the only family she had known.

During high school, Stephanie hung out with the wrong crowd and was in trouble most of the time. She got pregnant, but had a miscarriage, when she was 16. She loved to sing and dance. One of her teachers suggested to keep herself busy and to stay out of trouble, that she become involved with the drama club and the class productions, which were usually musicals. She landed some parts, and was pretty good, as she remembered. She also remembered how she decided to leave school when she turned 17. She went to New York City to pursue a career as a dancer. She had always dreamed of being a Rockette. But, with no professional training, it was just a dream. She did become a dancer, however, at The Pussycat, a strip club, and her life went downhill from there. Alcohol, drugs and an abusive boyfriend were not what she had anticipated.

Stephanie had met Frankie Salvatore at the club. She didn't know too much about his past, only that he was a bouncer, and he was supplying cocaine to most of the dancers. He was also involved in his uncle Mikey's business in New Jersey. He ran errands, made collections, and beat people up, when his uncle thought it was necessary. Stephanie and Frankie became friends and eventually moved in together.

To support their drug habits, some of the girls were doing sexual favors in the back of the club for whoever would pay them. Frankie knew what was going on, but since Stephanie was paying the rent, he let it slide. This situation lasted for over a year, until one night, the vice squad raided the club, and she and Frankie ended up in jail. Mikey bailed them out and brought them back to Lodi. He paid for her lawyer and her fines. She ended up working for the mob, and abusive Frankie was still her man. She felt trapped, but could see no way out.

As she now contemplated her past and what her future might bring, she lost track of where she was and missed the Route 80 exit. She was almost to Newark before she realized she had missed it. She took the next exit and drove around in circles before finding her way back onto the New Jersey Turnpike, headed back in the right direction. When she finally arrived back in Lodi, it was after 2:30 a.m., and Tata's was closed. She drove through the empty parking lot, and then headed a few blocks away to her apartment, which she and Frankie were currently sharing.

Stephanie parked the car and made her way up to the second floor apartment, an efficiency with one bedroom, one bathroom, a small kitchen and a den. She opened the door quietly, and entered. She looked to see if Frankie was asleep on the couch as he usually was when he wasn't out of town on "assignment" for Uncle Mikey, or sleeping at another woman's apartment. Tonight he was home, sprawled out on the couch in his underwear. There were four empty beer bottles on the coffee table next to him, along with an almost empty bottle of Jack Daniels. She made her way as quietly as possible into the kitchen, not wanting to wake him. She knew from past experience that he most likely was drunk and could get nasty in that condition. She needed to get a glass of water to take her pills that she took each night to help her relax and fall asleep. As she reached for a glass, her cat, a Siamese she called Tigger, came into the kitchen and brushed against her leg. This caused her to look down for a second, and as she did, she dropped the glass. She managed to catch it before it hit the counter, but it made a thud as she trapped it against the cabinet door.

"Shhh," she whispered to herself and Tigger. She drew some water from the faucet and took her pills out of a bottle on the window sill above the sink. She chugged down two pills, finished the water and turned around to go to the bedroom. Frankie blocked her way.

"Where the fuck you been?" he asked.

"Oh, hi," she said timidly. "You know, I was bringing that guy back to Long Island. Mikey asked me. You weren't around."

"For six fucking hours?" he roared.

"I got lost. I ended up past the airport. I Just got back."

"Right!" Frankie snarled. "What were you doin', blowin' him?"

She did not want to answer, knowing anything she might say could get him more fired up.

"Good night! You're drunk!" she replied, trying to move past him. "I'm going to bed." She picked up her cat off the floor, pushed by him, and started down the hall toward the bedroom. She heard him say "Bitch," and as she turned, she felt his big hand hit her beneath her right eye, knocking her on the floor. Tigger went flying, landed on its feet and scrambled into the bedroom. She started to crawl toward the bedroom door, hoping she could get in and lock it before he got to her. He was on her in a second, grabbing her by the hair. He pulled her up and knocked the door open, banging her face against the jamb. He dragged her in and threw her on the bed.

"No! Frankie! Get out!!" she screamed in pain, as he punched at her again. The blow just glanced off her shoulder, making him more angry,

"Fuck you! Get out!!" she yelled again.

"Fuck you? I'll fuck you!" he sneered as he fell on her yanking her skirt up to her waist. He tried to pin her down, but she squirmed and rolled toward the edge of the bed. He raised his hand and backhanded her across her brow, his big ring cutting her above the eye. Blood ran down her face as she tried to escape. He pulled her back and fell on her again. She felt his free hand between her legs ripping off her underwear. She tried desperately to resist, but he spread her legs apart. She knew the excitement of brutally controlling her had him aroused, and felt him entering her. After only a few quick thrusts, it was over. When he finally rolled off her, she quickly got out of bed and ran into the bathroom.

"Asshole!" she yelled, as she slammed the door and locked it. She knew he was too tired to respond and would soon be asleep. She turned on the bathroom light and looked at herself in the mirror. As she saw her battered face, she broke into tears. She knew she had to get out.

CHAPTER FIFTY-SIX

As Aldo walked up the driveway to his house , the security motion detector set off the lights illuminating the driveway. He could see skid marks on the pavement and tire tracks across the lawn and through the hedges. He wondered what had happened, but knew he had no way to find out. Both his wife and his friend were dead. He noticed that the garage door was open and wondered why. He went inside and turned on the lights. The basement garage looked basically the same as when he had left for their anniversary vacation. He noticed some of George's things, golf clubs, tennis rackets, tools laying around. Angie's car was in the other bay.

Aldo started up the stairs, wondering what he would find. At the top of the stairs, the door to the kitchen was open. He stepped inside and reached for the light switch where he remembered it would be. He flicked it on. The area was trashed. Drawers had been emptied onto the floor, fixtures and appliances were smashed, and glassware and broken bottles were everywhere. The refrigerator was open and spoiled food was strewn around the kitchen. "What the hell happened here?" he thought out loud.

Aldo stepped over items and walked into the den. The mess there was as bad as in the kitchen. Broken furniture and fixtures were everywhere. In one corner was a desk where their computer had been. The monitor was knocked on the floor, but the PC under the desk was apparently unnoticed by whomever trashed the place. He found the keyboard and touched it. The monitor came to life, awakening from its sleep mode. He turned it upright. On the screen was what looked like a travel itinerary.

4/16/99 Leave JFK 8:15a.m. Arrive Puerto Rico 12:35 p.m.

4/16/99 Leave Puerto Rico 2:50p.m. Arrive Anguilla 4:10 p.m.

Aldo thought back to that day and what had happened. He now knew why George and Angie had gone to Anguilla, and who had caused their demise. He still wondered if it all could have been prevented. He turned the recliner upright, sat down and fell asleep, exhausted.

CHAPTER FIFTY-SEVEN

Aldo woke to the sound of doorbell ringing. He realized where he was and shook the cobwebs from his head. He arose slowly and went to the window. He pulled back the curtain and peered out. It was morning and the sun was rising. There was a Syosset police car in his driveway and another parked on the street. Two officers were at his door. His first instinct was to run and hide, but then common sense told him that would be futile. He went to the door and slowly opened it. "Yes," Aldo said. "Can I help you?"

The young officer introduced himself and his partner. "I'm Officer Maillet and this is Officer Bnocchi from the Syosset Police Department."

Aldo knew this already from their nameplates and patrol car. "How can I help you?" he said.

"Is Mrs. Ferrari at home?" Maillet asked.

"No, she isn't."

"Well, who are you, and do you know where she is?" Bnocchi asked.

"I'm her husband, Aldo, and she's on vacation in the Caribbean, Anguilla. Is there a problem?"

"We've received a complaint about suspicious activity at this address, and we were sent to check it out. As a matter of fact, this is the second complaint in a week. On April 15th, last Tuesday night, there was a report of gunfire in the area. Were you aware of this?"

"No," Aldo replied. "I've been out of town for a while on business. Just got back last night."

"Is Mr. Macklin at home?" the officer then asked, startling Aldo.

"Who?" he said, quietly.

"Mr. George Macklin. He lists this as his primary residence."

Aldo thought for a moment. "Oh yeah, George. No, he's in the Caribbean," he paused. "With my wife," he said facetiously.

The officers looked at each other, surmising the situation. "I see," said Maillet. "So I suppose you're not too happy with that."

"Not at all," Aldo replied. "As a matter of fact. I'm filing for divorce immediately."

"Can you give us some ID that positively identifies you?" Officer Maillet asked.

"May we come in and look around?" Bnocchi said.

"Sure, hold on a minute," Aldo said. He went inside and realized he had nothing on him to prove he was Aldo Ferrari. All his documents said George Macklin. He went into the back room to where his desk used to be, hoping Angie had not gotten rid of all of his things. The desk was still there. He opened a few drawers but found only her things, and nothing to show he was her husband. Knowing the officers were waiting, he started to panic. Then he remembered the cabinet in the closet where they had kept a small, fireproof metal box with important documents, like birth certificates and mortgage papers. He hurried to check it out. He found the box, but it appeared locked. Not having time to look for the key, he threw it on the floor and it popped open, sprawling papers on the closet floor. He rummaged through them and found his old photo ID from his last job, his birth certificate, as well as an old driver's license and his marriage license. There was also a wedding picture of him and Angie.

Aldo hurried back to the living room where he saw the officers had already made their way into the house and were checking out the mess.

"Will this do? This is me and my wife, Mrs. Ferrari. Its 25 years ago, but you can see it's me, right? Here are some photo IDs. They're old, but you can see it's me."

Aldo could see the officers weren't convinced, so he changed the subject. "Look, check out how they trashed the place before they left. You should put out a warrant for their arrest for destroying my property."

Maillet said, "There is already a warrant out for Mr. Macklin by the Atlantic City Police in connection with a murder investigation. Would you know anything about that?"

Although Aldo quickly made the connection between this and what Stephanie and Mikey had told him, he replied, "No. Like I said, I've been away for a while."

After a brief consultation, Bnocchi said, "We'd like you to come down to the station to fill out a report so we can pursue this. We'll send a CSI unit out to look for evidence and maybe some clues to who trashed this place. You can file a formal complaint. Can you come now?"

"Well, I'm waiting for my luggage to arrive, they lost it on my flight back, but I will stop in later. Who should I ask for?"

Bnocchi handed him a card. "I will be there all afternoon," he said. "Don't make us come back for you."

"Sure, sure," Aldo acknowledged. "I'll see, you then. Thanks for helping. I really like to see this guy pay, the cheating bastard."

The officers turned and left. Aldo breathed a sigh of relief, but he knew this was only the beginning of more trouble. It would only be a matter of time before someone made the connection that Aldo Ferrari had died over a year ago. He had to run again!!

CHAPTER FIFTY-EIGHT

When the two officers arrived back at the precinct station, they passed by their commanding officer's office. "Hey, Maillet, come in here," said Sgt. Dick Condon, chief of detectives. "Did you get that Macklin guy?"

The two stepped in the office. "Uh, no, he wasn't there," Bnocchi said.

"Well, apparently, he was there, but he's gone now. He ran off with a Mrs. Ferrari. We talked to her husband, Aldo," said Maillet.

Condon thought a minute. "Wait a minute!" said the sergeant, looking perplexed. "Aldo Ferrari died over a year ago, drowned in the Caribbean, if I'm not mistaken. I remember because I play golf with his doctor."

"Uh, well, he showed us an ID. And he's coming down to fill out a report. Someone trashed his house."

"So you're saying you encountered a guy in a trashed house, didn't consider him a suspect because he showed you some ID, and let him go?" sneered the sergeant.

"Yeah, he seemed legit."

"Sure, he's legit. He showed you an ID of a guy that's been dead a year. Sounds legit to me. Get back there and get that guy, whoever he is. I want to talk to him," shouted Condon. "Maybe he knows where Macklin is."

"OK, sarge. Got it," Bnocchi said as they left the office.

After the two officers had gone, Detective Condon sat at his desk and thought about what his men had told him. After a while, he reached for the Rolodex on his desk and thumbed through it until he came to the listings under the letter I. Under insurance, he stopped and pulled out the card of Barbara Jakiela, claims investigator, with the firm of Girard and Jakiela, private investigators. He dialed the number listed first. After the third ring Ms. Jakiela answered.

"Hello, this is Barbara," she said.

"Hi, Barbara, Detective Condon from the Syosset Police Department calling."

"Oh, hi, Sergeant. How've you been?" she said cheerily. She had spoken with him on different occasions regarding cases she was investigating in his area. Her firm investigated insurance fraud for major companies.

"Just fine," said Condon." I have a question about a file I recall you might have worked on, about a year ago. Do you recall the Ferrari case?"

"Ferrari? Oh, yes, we did that for Northwestern. The guy drowned out in the Caribbean."

"Anything unusual that you can remember?" he asked.

"No, pretty simple case as I can remember. Everything checked out. Death certificates, police reports from the island, and all that. The only thing suspicious, or I should say, unusual," she continued, "was that the policy was only in force for a short while when the accident happened. But the company paid his widow a nice sum, half a million, as I recall. Why do you ask?"

"Well," Condon replied, "a couple of my officers ran into a guy who passed himself off as Ferrari, even showed them IDs."

"No kidding," Barbara said. "And where did they run into him?"

"At his house, over in Muttontown."

"Is that so?"

"Yeah, there on their way back there now to bring him down here for questioning."

"Well, keep me informed if anything happens. We could still reopen the case, if Northwestern wants to pursue it."

"Sure enough, Barbara. Thanks. Take care of yourself."

Condon hung up. He then made a call to his golfing buddy, Dr. Phil Mangio.

"Doctor Mangio's office. Can I help you?" the receptionist said.

"Hi, Cindy. Dick Condon. Is Phil in?" Condon asked.

"Hello, Detective, how are you?" Before he could answer she said, "Could you hold a minute?" and he heard a click and then some "elevator music." He started getting impatient when she came back on the line.

"Sorry, Dick, he will be right with you. Did he forget his tee time again?" Cindy asked.

"No, I would just like to ask him a question."

"OK, have a nice day. Here he is." The phone clicked again.

"Hey, Detective, what's up?" the good doctor asked his friend.

"My men were over in Muttontown this morning and questioned a guy who claims he is Aldo Ferrari. Wasn't he a patient of yours at one time?" Condon asked.

"Yes, nice guy," Mangio replied. "But he died over a year ago, fell off a cliff when he and his wife were on vacation in the Caribbean."

"That's what I thought. Who could this guy be? He was at Ferrari's house. Showed some IDs. What about a George Macklin? Know anything about him?"

"Sure. He and Aldo were best buddies. When Aldo died, George moved in with his wife. I heard he was having some financial problems, probably because of his gambling. He had lost his wife a few years back. She drowned, too, in her pool. Some people thought that was a little suspicious, since they never got along. I met him a few times. Never really liked him."

"That's interesting," Condon said. "If somehow this is Ferrari, could you positively identify him? You know, birthmarks or something."

"Well, you know about patient privacy and all that. But since he is supposed to be dead, I guess I could be of help in an investigation."

"Ok, thanks, Phil. See you tomorrow at the club. Try not to be late. I don't care, but that asshole McGirk gets bent out of shape when he has to wait five seconds."

"OK, fine. But the madder he is, the worse he plays. Take care."

Condon hung up the phone with more to think about. Maybe it could have been Macklin his men talked to and there was a warrant out for his arrest.

CHAPTER FIFTY-NINE

In New Jersey, Mikey got a phone call from one of his people whom he had sent to keep tabs on Aldo until he could be sure he could trust him, or at least until he had his 200 g's back.

"What's goin on?" asked the shark.

"Well, the cops were at your new friend's house for an hour this morning."

"No kidding. Anything happen?"

"No," said the informer. "The cops left, Ferrari's still there."

"OK, stay outta sight and keep an eye on him." Mike hung up.

"What's up, boss?" asked Frankie Salvatore, who had overheard the conversation.

"Our boy's been talkin to the cops. Maybe this relationship's not gonna turn out so good. We gotta get the money soon and then decide what to do with him. See if you can get you and him on a plane to San Juan tonight."

"Sure, boss."

CHAPTER SIXTY

Aldo quickly rummaged through the house, looking for anything he might use to help him as he fled the police and the mob. He found the keys to Angie's car, a bank account passbook, an ATM card, which he hoped was still valid. Fumbling around he came across the keys to the Macklin Funeral Home. He knew he had to leave the house soon, and figured he could hide out there if he had to.

He gathered some of George's clothes and put them in a duffle bag. He went down to the garage and got into Angie's car. After a few cranks of the engine, it started. He drove out of the garage, closed the door with the remote and left. As he drove out of the driveway, he looked around the street to see if any suspicious vehicles were parked nearby, but, since he had been way from the area for a while, he realized that he would not be able to tell if a vehicle was suspicious or not. There was only one car parked on the street a few houses away, and no one appeared to be in it.

As Aldo drove out of his street and onto a main thoroughfare, a squad car passed, going in the opposite direction. Aldo surmised Maillet and Bnocchi had not noticed him as they passed. But, he had recognized them, and his heart raced a little faster. He knew they were going back to get him. He thought about going directly to a bank to get some cash, but he knew he would be recorded by the surveillance cameras, and so he decided to try to get by with what he had until he could get to Puerto Rico and recover the money he had left there. He headed for the funeral home. Maybe there was something of value there. Anyhow, it could be a place to hide until he could decide on his next move.

Aldo parked a few blocks from Macklin's and walked to the facility. He didn't know what or who he would find there. Unfortunately, he knew that George had not been there for a few weeks and wouldn't be coming back. He thought about George lying on that beach, beaten and shot dead. He didn't deserve that, Aldo thought, but then again, maybe he did. He strolled past the building, checking it out, and it seemed deserted. He went around to the side door, where he couldn't be seen from the street and tried a key. It did not work. He tried two more on the ring and the latch opened. He quickly went inside. He made his way through the dimly lit rooms, the only light coming from a transom above the door and a security night-light. He went down a hallway to where he remembered the office was. The door was locked, but after a few tries, he located the correct key and opened it. He entered the office. It had a number of windows so there was plenty of light.

Although Aldo didn't know what he was looking for or what he would find, but he began going through the desk drawers. After looking at a lot of papers he knew nothing about, he finally found something he recognized. It was the letter he had sent George from Anguilla. He did get it, Aldo thought, but still wondered why they had to go there, and wished they had not.

In a file cabinet, he found records of burials and cremations. He paused a moment before going to the year and month he had "died." He shuffled more papers and finally found his death file. A notarized death certificate and insurance papers were in the file, along with the record of his cremation. How did they pull this off without a body, he wondered. As he was contemplating his own death, he heard a noise, which seemed to come from downstairs in the mortuary. It startled him. It sounded like something had been knocked over. He went over to the window, from where he could see the parking lot, but did not see any cars.

It was just beginning to get dark outside and, as it did, the interior of the building was becoming dimmer. Because did not want to put on the lights, he moved slowly out of the office and down the stairs, trying to keep in the shadows.

Since there were no windows in the mortuary, he thought he would turn on the lights, if he could remember where the switch was and could find it without running into something, or worse, somebody. He always thought this was an eerie place when he would come here to visit George, but now alone in the dark, it was much scarier. There even may be a body or two in the cooler. He had no idea how fast George had fled or in what state he had left his business.

As Aldo moved along the wall, feeling for the light switch, he brushed against something that made him recoil. It felt like bones! His breathing stopped until he remembered the life-sized skeleton George kept there. It wasn't real, just a replica that George had picked up at a medical supply house clearance sale. George thought it would be a fun thing to have in the mortuary. Right now, Aldo didn't think it was funny. He continued searching for the lights. He came to a corner and hesitated. He thought he could feel the presence of another person nearby. He reached around the corner, touched something, someone, and heard an ear shattering scream, a woman's scream. He reached again, felt the light switch and flicked it on. Stephanie DiNuzzo stared back at him.

"What!" Aldo started. "What the hell are you doing here?" he yelled.

On seeing Aldo, Stephanie let out a sigh of relief, and said. "They sent me to find you, give you a message. They have been trying to get in touch with you. They want you to go to San Juan tonight, with Frankie."

"How did you find me here?" Aldo asked.

"I saw you as you were leaving the house. I followed you. Shit! I didn't know you were coming to this, this creepy place."

"Well, you scared the crap out of me, too."

Looking at her bruises and swollen eye, he asked. "What the hell happened to your face?"

"Uh, Frankie got mad when I got home late last night," she replied.

"Jesus, you look terrible!"

"I know, sorry," she said softly. "Anyway, you're supposed to be at Newark at 10:30 tonight. Supposed to fly to San Juan, get the money and come back as soon as you can. Frankie will meet you there, at the airport. I got his number to call him."

Aldo rubbed his chin, not liking that idea at all. "I don't think I like that plan. So forget you ever saw me, OK?"

"I don't know," Stephanie said, sounding worried. "What are you going to do? You better be careful!"

"I'm not sure. But thanks for the advice. I plan on being careful."

"Good. Um, can I help you? I don't really want to go back and tell them I didn't see you. Somehow, they will know I'm lying."

"That's your problem. Besides, I got this feeling that you being with me could turn out to be dangerous, for both of us."

"That's OK, it can't be worse than the situation I'm in now. It's like they own me. Look at me, for Christ sake. I got to get away, now, somehow."

"Well, you put yourself in that situation," he told her.

"Yeah, I guess, but maybe, together, we can both get out. Two heads are better than one. Please, Aldo, I need you," she pleaded.

Aldo thought that although he didn't need an anchor, she might be helpful with information about his pursuers. Also, she sounded desperate. After a long silence, he said, "Come on, let's get out of here. They may be watching you, too."

CHAPTER SIXTY-ONE

Aldo and Stephanie walked back to Aldo's car, looking around as they went, checking that no one was following them. They got in and drove off.

"Where we going?" DiNuzzo asked.

"I don't know if I should tell you," Aldo said. "You might call your friends in New Jersey and let them know. I still don't know if I can trust you."

"They're not my, well, they were my friend's, but I'm not gonna call them. Believe me, please, Aldo. You're my chance to get away. Maybe start a new life. I know it's hard for you to trust me, but, gimme a chance. I promise you won't be sorry!"

Aldo thought she sounded sincere, but felt he still didn't know her. She could be acting. "We are getting out of here, that's all you need to know."

Aldo knew he had to get back to San Juan to retrieve the money as quickly as he could, before they could set up surveillance there, if they hadn't already. He knew they would be checking local airports, JFK, La Guardia, and Newark, so he decided to make a run north to Bradley International, just north of Hartford, Connecticut. Barring heavy traffic, they could be there in about two hours. He thought that American Airlines ran flights out of there daily to San Juan, and with the police and the mob after them, it seemed like a safer place to hide than the New York area. They exited Long Island, went across the Whitestone Bridge and headed up I-95 north. In New Haven, they took I-91 north and arrived at the airport about 9:30 p.m. He parked at the curb, asking Stephanie to wait while he arranged for tickets.

Aldo went to the American Airlines desk and found that the last flight to San Juan had left 30 minutes earlier. The next one was at 6:45 a.m. He bought two tickets for that flight, went back to the car and told Stephanie they were getting a room for a few hours.

"Sure, whatever, you decide. I'm with you. Aint you lucky?"

He didn't even smile. He had too much on his mind. He knew Mikey would be after him as soon as they didn't hear from him or Dinuzzo, and the Syosset police also would be looking for him.

"Maybe this wasn't a good idea. Maybe he should go back. Maybe he shouldn't trust his new friend," he thought.

Since the flight was a very early, he decided to stay at the hotel in the airport terminal complex. They checked into the Sheraton, paying cash to avoid any paper trail. They were both starved, so they picked up sandwiches from the only restaurant still open in the complex, went to their room and settled in for the night. Stephanie tried to explain to Aldo about her past, and how she got mixed up with Frankie and his uncle Mikey. He felt some sympathy for her, but knew he had his own problems to figure out. After eating, Stephanie took a pill and dozed off as soon as she hit the bed. Aldo showered and tried to sleep. Eventually he nodded off.

CHAPTER SIXTY-TWO

At midnight, a call came into the American Airlines reservations call center. "American Airlines, this is Lindsey, how can I help you?" the clerk asked.

"Hi, this is Aldo Ferrari. I would like to confirm my reservation. My secretary made them for me, and I can't get in touch with her now. Could you help me?"

"Sure sir, could you spell your last name?"

"F E R R A R I."

"Just a minute, sir, I'll look that up."

After a short pause, Lindsey came back on the line. "Sir, I show an Aldo Ferrari booked on Flight 2215, leaving Bradley International at 6:45 a.m., on the 22nd, that's this morning."

"Thank you very much," the man said.

"You're welcome, sir. Anything else I can help you with this evening."

The phone caller hung up. At the time Aldo was asleep in his room.

CHAPTER SIXTY-THREE

At 5:30 a.m., Aldo nudged Stephanie from her sleep. "Let's go," he said.

"What? Go?" she replied, still half-asleep.

"Well, I'm getting on a plane in an hour. You can come with me or go back to sleep, it's your call." She rose slowly and stumbled into the bathroom.

They grabbed coffee in the hotel lobby and headed down the concourse toward the terminal. After a short walk, they passed through security and looked for Gate six. They arrived at their gate and waited to board. Two men, sitting across the lobby, watched them intently as they presented their tickets and boarded the plane.

Flight 2215 arrived in San Juan on schedule at 10:50 a.m. Aldo and Stephanie left the plane under watchful eyes. Even though those following them tried to be inconspicuous, Aldo knew he was being watched.

"Where we going?" DiNuzzo asked.

"Just keep close," Aldo said, as they walked down the concourse. They went in this shop and that store, trying to lose their pursuers, and finally stopped at a small cafe and sat down at a table in the corner. He had to figure out how to get to the locker, where the cash and handgun were stored, without being followed. He pulled out his wallet to be sure the small locker key he had put there two days earlier was still there. He motioned for Stephanie to come closer, and he whispered to her. "Don't turn around fast, but there are two men out there that are tailing us. You recognize them?"

She turned slowly and looked out the cafe window. "The ones near the news stand?" she asked.

"Yeah, the guys in the suits"

"No, they don't look like anyone I know."

As she stared at the men, another man walked by the café window. "Oh, my God!!" she whispered to Aldo. "It's Frankie!!"

"Who?"

"Frankie, my boyfriend, ex-boyfriend. The one I told you about last night. He just walked by."

Frankie hadn't stopped, continuing down the concourse, obviously looking for someone.

Aldo thought for a second. "Calm down. You got a lighter?" he asked.

"Sure. Why?"

"I know this sounds scary, and may be crazy, but I want you to go into the ladies room out there and light a fire in the trash can. Just start it and leave. Don't come back here. Meet me at the other side of the terminal, where we got off the plane." He paused." Can you do it?"

She looked at him as if he had three eyes and then said, "Yeah, I guess so."

"We need a diversion to lose these guys, while I get the money. I hope that will do it," he said, almost as if he did not believe it would. "OK, go!" he told her.

She got up, looking scared.

"Hey, be careful. We'll be all right," he said as he touched her arm.

"Yeah, sure," she mumbled as she walked away.

The men watched her as she left the restaurant and walked to the rest room a short distance away. From where they were standing, they could see where she went and so they turned their attention back to Aldo. He sat patiently waiting for her to do her deed. A busboy came to his table and starting collecting their glasses. Aldo pulled out a $20 bill and said to the kid, "You speak English?"

"Yes sir," the boy said.

"Sit down here a second," Aldo said as he handed the kid the $20 and pulled out another one. "I want to buy your hat. Is this enough?"

The boy's eyes lit up as he saw the cash. "Si, sure," he said looking around for his boss.

The alarms went off, as smoke hit the detectors in the ladies' room. People started looking around for an escape route, if there was indeed a fire. When smoke started coming out of the rest room, panic erupted. Aldo grabbed the kid's hat, as well as his bus pan and headed for the kitchen.

Security police rushed toward the rest room, past the men who were tailing Aldo, temporarily distracting them. When they looked back into the cafe, Aldo was gone. He was in the kitchen looking for a back door. Because of the commotion outside, and his flimsy disguise, no one paid any attention to him. He saw a door marked "Emergency Exit." It was in Spanish, but he figured it out quickly and pushed it open. He was in a dirty hallway, cluttered with trash barrels and mops and other cleaning gear. He moved along until he saw another exit door and made his way through it. He was back out on the concourse. He wasn't exactly sure where, but took a chance and turned left. He could hear the commotion from the area of the fire, and kept moving away from it. He turned a corner and realized that he had gotten lucky. Just down the way was the bank of lockers he was looking for. He sprinted over and found the locker where he had left the satchel. He retrieved the key from his pocket. He glanced around, opened the small door, grabbed the bag and headed off to find Stephanie.

CHAPTER SIXTY-FOUR

iNuzzo had gone into the restroom. There were two other women there, talking in front of a mirror. She didn't hesitate, and went right to the trash receptacle. She grabbed some paper towels from a dispenser, turned her back to the other ladies, took out her lighter and ignited them. She dropped the burning paper into the trash. The other women saw the smoke and fire and screamed and headed for the door. Stephanie followed close behind, so close that the three looked inseparable.

Outside, in the hall, Stephanie moved quickly and tried to get lost in the panicking crowd. She tried to remember at which gate they had exited the plane. She thought it was gate 16 and started down the concourse that she thought she and Aldo had come from. People were pushing and shoving in an attempt to get away from the smoking rest room. She wondered where Aldo had gone and if she would ever see him again. Then she saw a sign for gates 12 -18. She was on the right track, she thought. Then, a hand reached out and grabbed her arm, squeezing it tightly. She turned. It was Frankie.

"Nice to see you, bitch," he sneered at her. "Thought you lost me, didn't you?"

"No, let go of me!" she yelled, trying to pull away. He squeezed her arm tighter.

"Help!!" she screamed, trying to attract attention. Those around them were trying to find the nearest exit and ignored her.

"Where's your pal?" he shouted in her ear.

"Who? I don't know!" she cried, wincing in pain from his strong grip on her arm.

"You know. Tell me or I will break your arm off!" he snarled, squeezing tighter.

"Ow! Stop! OK, he's down this way somewhere," she replied, motioning toward gate 16.

"Let's go!" he said, and pushed her down the hallway.

CHAPTER SIXTY-FIVE

When Aldo arrived at the Gate 16 waiting area, it was deserted. He found a spot in the corner of the room where he could see someone coming, but they could not see him until they got close. He wasn't going to wait for long. If Stephanie didn't show up soon, she was on her own. He still had no plan for getting out of there, but he knew the sooner the better.

It was only a few minutes later when Aldo saw Frankie and Stephanie heading toward him. Frankie had a grip on her arm and was pushing her along. Aldo moved behind a large sign advertising Ray-Ban sunglasses and thought about his next move. Then he remembered the 9mm that was under the money in the satchel he was carrying. He tried to remember if he had left it loaded. He opened the bag and grabbed the gun just as Frankie and Stephanie neared. When they were alongside Aldo's hiding spot, he stepped out and pointed the gun directly at Frankie's head. "Let her go!" he shouted at him.

Surprised, Frankie pulled her closer. She tried to pull away, but he now had his arm around her shoulder using her as a shield. He then pulled a small switchblade from his jacket, snapped it open and held it against her throat.

"Let her go!" Aldo said again. "I'll shoot."

"No fucking way," Frankie replied. "Put the gun down and

she won't get hurt." They stood six feet from each other in a gut-wrenching stand off.

Stephanie had one free arm and she boldly jabbed her elbow into Frankie's ribcage. He flinched, and loosened his grip on her, but still held on. She tried to pull away again, and as she did, Aldo had a clear shot at Frankie's legs. He pointed the gun and pulled the trigger, hoping it was still loaded. The bullet ripped through Frankie's knee.

"Ahh! You fucker!!" he shouted, looking down at his leg and lowering the knife. Stephanie took this chance to pull away from him. He tried to grab her and Aldo fired again hitting the other leg. Frankie fell to the floor, writhing in pain.

Aldo picked up the satchel, grabbed Stephanie and looked for the closest door. It was next to the attendant's desk and they headed for it. Stephanie looked back at Frankie lying on the floor and stopped. She turned around and walked back to him. He was trying to get up. She moved close and kicked him, knocking him back down. He sprawled out on his back, and she brought her leg back and kicked him solidly in the groin. "Fuck you, Frankie!" she yelled at him as he moaned in pain. "Fuck you!!" she shouted again as she ran to catch up with Aldo. He was headed to the door which led to the boarding ramp. He opened it and they ran down the ramp. There was no plane waiting at the end. Aldo pushed open the door that led to the tarmac below. An alarm went off as the door opened, and they climbed down the portable ladder.

Many people were outside on the tarmac. The terminal was being evacuated because of the fire, and their escaping down the ladder did not draw much attention.

After they descended the ladder, they tried to mingle with the crowd. Aldo cautiously tried to survey the people around them, looking for the two men that had been watching them in the terminal. He spotted one of them moving briskly among the crowd, obviously looking for someone. Aldo nudged Stephanie in the other direction and they moved away toward some hangars and disappeared between two buildings.

CHAPTER SIXTY–SIX

On one section of the huge airport, there was an area for private aircraft. A number of small planes were lined up in rows, waiting for their owner-pilots to fly off to some island destination. John Faulkner, a former Navy fighter pilot, was on a ladder, working on the engine of a small Piper Cub. He was 43 years old and had left the service because of medical problems, mostly drug related. He now did odd jobs around the airport, occasionally flying mainly for beer and drug money. He was unshaven and wore dirty cutoff jeans and an old U.S. Navy T-shirt. He had a chaw of tobacco in his mouth. His hands and arms were greasy from the plane he was servicing. He looked down to see Aldo and Stephanie staring up at him. "What's up?" he asked. "You lost?"

"You might say that," Aldo said. "Can you fly this thing?"

Faulkner chuckled. "I can fly anything."

"What about that one?" Aldo asked, pointing to a Cessna Caravan Amphibian, three spots away from where they were. It was a seaplane and Aldo figured it would be better for landing near a small island. No runway was needed.

"Sure," Faulkner said. "No problem."

"But can you land it?" Aldo shot back.

"That's funny," the pilot said. "Piece of cake. Why do you ask?"

"We got to get out of here, get to Anguilla," Aldo said as he reached in the satchel and took out a stack of $100 bills. "This is yours, if you can get us there."

Faulkner's eyes widened. He stared at the cash for a few seconds, and said. "OK, I got to talk to someone about using the plane. File a flight plan. Come back in an hour."

Aldo pulled out another stack. "We got to go now!" he said.

Faulkner came down the ladder to get a closer look at the money. He spit a stream of brown saliva onto the tarmac. He scratched his head. "Now, huh?" he mumbled.

"Now!" Aldo said.

"Come on," the pilot said as he walked toward the seaplane. He checked the door of the Cessna to make sure it was unlocked. Then he pulled down the portable stairs and motioned for Aldo and Stephanie to climb aboard. He then went under the aircraft to remove the chocks from under the wheels and check other mechanical details. Stephanie went up but just as Aldo started to climb the stairs he felt something in his back. Martin Alvarez pushed his handgun into Aldo's ribs and said, "Goin somewhere, Senor?" Alvarez, Mikey "the Sharks" new Caribbean hit man, had also been following the two runaways. He was supposed to connect with Frankie, but by the time he found him, Frankie was helpless, lying on the floor with both legs shot out. Frankie had told him how his girl and Aldo had escaped, and Martin had gone to the window in time to see them outside on the tarmac hurrying away.

Aldo turned around and faced his old nemesis. "Martin, nice to see you again," he said facetiously. "I thought we had settled our differences, became friends. What's with the gun?"

"Well, my friend, I guess you have something there that doesn't belong to you," Martin said, pointing toward the satchel in Aldo's hand. "I just came to get it back."

"And if I won't give it back?" Aldo asked.

"Then I will have to keel you, and your friend there, too," Martin replied, looking up toward Stephanie, who was standing in the doorway of the plane.

"Maybe we can work this out, give you a share. There's a lot to share," Aldo pleaded.

"No deals," Martin shouted. "Give me it!"

Martin reached for the satchel and, as he did, Faulkner hit him square on the head with a large tire iron. Blood spurted from Martin's scalp as he fell to the ground.

Faulkner picked up Martin's gun, spit again and asked, "Who the hell is this?"

"One of the reasons we got to get out of here, now. There may be more like him on the way"

"Let's go!" the pilot said as he scrambled aboard behind Aldo.

As the Cessna started to move, the radio aboard squawked out a message. "ALL DEPARTURES FROM THIS AIRPORT ARE TEMPORARILY SUSPENDED. ALL AIRCRAFT PLEASE HOLD YOUR POSITION UNTIL FURTHER NOTICE."

"What the hell is that all about?" Faulkner exclaimed.

"Probably has something to do with the fire in the terminal," Aldo said. "But we must go now!"

Aldo flashed the money in front of Faulkner, "No go, no cash."

Faulkner turned the plane onto the closest runway and maneuvered it around four jumbo jets waiting for clearance for takeoff. He picked up speed once he reached the open track. Just then, a large service vehicle started to pull out onto the runway in an apparent attempt to block their takeoff. It was a fuel tanker truck. Two security police cars were behind it.

The plane accelerated and sped toward the huge truck. Stephanie screamed as Faulkner pulled back on the joystick and the plane's nose pulled up. The plane grazed the top of the truck with a slight thud. Sparks flew and the tanker exploded in a huge fireball. The Cessna escaped through the flames and climbed into the sky and out over the Atlantic. "Yahoo!!" yelled Faulkner. "Just like Nam!!"

CHAPTER SIXTY-SEVEN

Forty minutes later, several children were playing on the beach near the village Aldo had left a few days earlier. They looked up as a plane circled around, closing in on the inlet. Faulkner had kept the plane low in order to stay under any radar and had made a number of course changes as they made their way toward the island. He knew the authorities would surely be looking for them, after the commotion they had caused at the airport.

Faulkner still wasn't sure how much damage to his landing gear he had sustained on takeoff. He said to Aldo, "Here. Hold this steady. I'm gonna hang out and check the pontoons."

"Sure," Aldo said, having no idea what he was doing.

"Just hold this steady," Faulkner instructed. The plane headed back out over the ocean. Faulkner opened the side door and laid on the floor of the plane. He edged himself out as far as possible, leaned over, and peered under the plane. He came back in.

"A little damage to the left one. If we come in leaning to the right, we should be all right."

Stephanie swallowed hard.

Faulkner sat back at the controls, turned the plane back towards the inlet and started his descent. "Here we go!" he shouted. "Hang on!"

The plane came down on the smooth sea and started to tip left. Faulkner pushed on the joystick, and the nose of the plane nearly went in the water. Everyone lurched forward, but the plane came to a stop and settled on the calm inlet.

Aldo emerged from the plane and stood on the wing. He spotted Melky on the shore and motioned for him to get in his boat and come out. Melky looked out at them and seemed astonished to see Aldo again. He then got in the boat with two other boys and started out.

As Aldo and Stephanie waited for their ride to shore, Faulkner came out onto the wing, obviously looking for payment for his services. Aldo reached into the satchel, took out one bundle of bills, put it in his own pocket and threw the bag with the rest of the cash to the pilot. "Here, keep the rest," he said. "You deserve it, and probably will need it more than we will."

Faulkner grinned broadly, revealing tobacco stained teeth. "Yep, probably will," he replied as he looked toward shore and the peaceful little village.

Stephanie also looked to shore and then at the satchel full of cash. She considered her situation. "So, where you going?" she asked Faulkner.

"I don't know, but if I can get this thing up in the air, I'm going to hide somewhere."

"Want some company, I got to hide too," she said, giving him a sexy stare.

Faulkner stared back. "I usually don't like company, but, sure. Let's go."

Stephanie looked at Aldo lovingly and moved closer. "It's been fun. Thanks, but I don't think I'd be happy here," she said, glancing toward shore. She put her arms around him and hugged him warmly. She kissed him, turned and got into the cockpit.

"Be safe. Be happy," Aldo replied, and stepped off the wing into Melky's boat. "Take care of her!" he shouted at Faulkner as the boat moved away.

The Cessna's engine roared to life. The seaplane turned and accelerated across the water and finally rose up into the sky.

Aldo waved as the plane turned, came back and passed overhead. He then looked toward the shore and the peaceful village. This could be the beginning of his new life, he thought, a good life, for perhaps the rest of his life. But as he watched the plane soar off along the coastline, he caught sight of the cliffs where this misadventure had started. He thought about Angie falling to her death, and George, who was brutally murdered. "Why did he himself survive?" he wondered. "Wasn't he the one who wanted to die?"

Again guilt overcame him, and once again he contemplated going back, back to the edge.

THE END

EPILOGUE

Aldo Ferrari was once again welcomed by the villagers. He returned to the laid back life style he had enjoyed before he left to seek out answers to the questions he had concerning his wife, Angie, and his friend, George. His feelings of guilt eventually subsided as he realized there was little more he could have done to protect his wife from George, who had committed murder and was planning to kill both he and Angie.

Aldo was content to stay there in that peaceful place for the rest of his days. Unfortunately, that would not be for very long. A few months after arriving there his stomach problem got much worse and, although he continued taking the elixir the elder had given him, he soon became very ill. He considered going to the hospital in The Valley or returning to the United States for treatment, but remembered Dr. Mangio's prognosis and realized now that the doctor was most likely correct. Aldo passed away ten months after returning to the island.

Before he died, he was visited by John Faulkner and Stephanie. They had ditched the seaplane on St. Kitts soon after leaving Aldo and purchased a sailboat with the money Aldo had given them. They had traveled the Caribbean from island to island for a while and then decided to go to Anguilla to check on Aldo. They found him on his deathbed. Before he died, Aldo gave them information about

Angie's bank accounts and the house on Long Island. In return, they promised to bury him at sea when he passed away, so he could once again be with Angie. After fulfilling that promise, Faulkner and DiNuzzo, who had become lovers, sailed off in search of new treasures. But that's another story.

Disclaimer

This book is a work of fiction. Any resemblance to actual events, locales, or persons, living or dead, is coincidental. Names, characters, places and incidents are a product of the author's imagination or are used fictitiously.

My apologies to the good people of Anguilla for taking liberties with the history of their beautiful island.

Acknowledgements

I would like to thank my family and friends who encouraged and supported me in the writing of this novel, especially my wife Rae, son Rick, and daughters Ranee and Robbin, whose love and support I will always cherish.

Also, special thanks to Barbara, Beverly, Joyce, Lindsey, Mary Ann, Rosemary, Melanie, Donna, Marie, Debbie, Amira and all those who pre-read this work and encouraged me to continue. Thanks also to my editor, Roberta J. Buland of Right Words Unlimited, who guided me through the editing and publishing process.